CLARE
SILCOCK.

The River Boy

THERESA WHISTLER

The River Boy

WITH AN INTRODUCTION BY
LORD DAVID CECIL

Illustrated by
Richard Shirley-Smith

London
OXFORD UNIVERSITY PRESS
1976

Oxford University Press

OXFORD LONDON GLASGOW NEW YORK TORONTO MELBOURNE WELLINGTON
CAPE TOWN IBADAN NAIROBI DAR ES SALAAM LUSAKA ADDIS ABABA
DELHI BOMBAY CALCUTTA MADRAS KARACHI LAHORE DACCA
KUALA LUMPUR SINGAPORE HONG KONG TOKYO

ISBN 0 19 271382 5

© Theresa Whistler 1976

The story *The River Boy* was first published
by Rupert Hart-Davis, London, 1955

This edition first published 1976
by Oxford University Press

*Printed in Great Britain by offset lithography by
Billing & Sons Ltd, Guildford, London and Worcester*

For
DANIEL

CONTENTS

Introduction

C. S. Lewis says in *Of Other Worlds* that the test of a good children's book is that it is also enjoyed by grown-up people. If *Alice in Wonderland* and Hans Andersen's tales pass this test, so surely does *The River Boy*. It is a fantasy about a fatherless only child called Nat living in the country and much concerned with country things: trees, flowers and especially animals, wild and tame. The story tells how he meets with a visionary playmate whom he calls the river boy and who is at once a sort of reflection of himself and an elfin being, gifted with mysterious powers. The river boy takes him into a countryside resembling the one he lives in but magical and different, and containing a river which the river boy knows all about but which is new to Nat. Together the two boys set out to follow its downward course and their journey involves them in various strange and thrilling adventures and misadventures. These adventures take place as it were 'out of time'. The story is interspersed with passages 'in time' and in the real world where Nat continues to pursue his ordinary way of life.

The trouble with tales of this kind is usually that the author fails to do equal justice to both strains in his conception. Seldom is his tale equally convincing as fantasy and as reality. Not so *The River Boy*. The fantasy is wholly and fascinatingly convincing; sometimes thrilling, as when Nat catches sight of the river boy skimming with strange blank gaze over the surface of the twilit water; sometimes ecstatic, as in the vision of the shadowless tower rising bathed in light above stretches of golden cornfield; sometimes comical and whimsical, as in the description of Nat's supper in the Miller's house, consisting as it does partly of mushrooms fried in a gold-framed mirror and of a salad like a garden with a fountain of oil and vinegar playing in the midst of it. But the realistic side of the book is equally convincing. Nat is a living flesh and blood boy, and the countryside he lives in, its trees and flowers and weather and animals are described in a way that shows an extraordinary close and accurate observation of the English scene. Nor is there any sense of jar as we move from the real to the fantastic and back again. They are fused together; so that the real reinforces the fantasy and the fantasy irradiates the real. The result is a human story which is also a poetic daydream.

No wonder that it has an appeal both to children and their elders. They may indeed react to it differently. The children are likely to enjoy it simply as a story that takes their imagination. Their elders, on the other hand, may suspect that it would not hold them as it does if it were not fraught with some deeper significance: alike its general gist and many of its particular incidents seem resonant with symbolic overtones. Like all good symbols these are not to be defined precisely. Does the river stand for the River of Life leading Nat from childhood to maturity? Is the shadowless tower an image of celestial bliss for which the soul is ever searching? Is the death in the real world of the old horse Rose followed by the appearance in the visionary world of the young horse, radiant in its whiteness, a metaphor for death and resurrection as facts of human destiny?

Such questions inevitably force themselves into the mind of the grown-up reader. But he should not pay too much attention to them. *The River Boy* is not a precisely thought-out heavyweight allegory. Rather it is an iridescent bubble of fancy which, though streaked with shadows of a deeper mystery, is yet designed first of all to delight children.

As I know from experience, it succeeds in doing this; and even the appeal it has for their elders comes primarily from the fact that it transports them imaginatively back to childhood and to childhood's airborne daydreams.

DAVID CECIL
1976

The River Boy

ONE

To Get into One's Head

NATHANIEL lived as a child in a house called Bourne that stood
in a wreath of dark woods, not quite upon a hill-top, but in the
saddle between two crests. To one side the land slanted gently
away in fields and neglected cherry-orchards, and climbed
again to a ridge where a village straggled behind its small,
severe church, like a string of goslings behind a grey goose.
There Nathaniel would trudge each day to school. On the other
side of Bourne the woods fell steeply to a deep and narrow
green valley, where rushes grew and yellow flags; and in winter
broad puddles shone across it, but no water ran.

It looked like a river valley. One expected to find, somewhere,
at least the plaited twinkle of a stream among the rushes; but
if there ever had been one it had long since sunk underground,
and all its kingfishers and herons had flown away. Nathaniel
had explored it almost a mile each way, but always the steep
woods hung above his head, and the valley wound emptily

between. He wondered if there had been a water-course there in the far-off days when his father had been a boy; but his mother did not know, and his father was dead.

On windy nights in his attic bedroom he would start up out of sleep crying, 'I *knew* it was there!' because the wind in the yew-trees had woven itself into his dreams as the sound of a weir. And at times Nathaniel wearied of the large, old-fashioned house, friendly but very silent. Even the beautiful walled garden, half overgrown with evening primroses, seemed drearily landlocked, thirsty, and deadly still.

His life was a solitary one, for no children of his own age lived nearer than the village, and Nathaniel was given to day-dreams. Often he fell into one that was little more than a kind of waiting and listening for someone, he knew not who, to come. There were times when the contented hiss of drying logs, or the click of the sinking coals, seemed to take on a special tone just before bedtime, and talk to him of this unknown companion's coming. Then the idle wind in the chimney began to talk of it too, and it always seemed to Nathaniel that if only he had not been called away to bed just then, in a moment more he would have understood what they were saying. Then sometimes the catch of the little window at the top of the stairs would cry faintly in the night air, when he shuffled along the corridor in his slippers, as if it were trying to tell him some secret of the enormous country darkness outside. It was calling his attention away from the ordinariness of bathtime and bed. Then, as he stood still for a moment, with vacant stare fixed on the candle-flame as it grew taller and taller, trembling in the draught, it would seem to Nathaniel that he had been on the very point of meeting someone, and had missed the chance by a mere fraction of a second. The window-catch had cried out to warn him, but he had not listened quite in time. Whoever it was had passed by.

Once he was lying in the sunshine on the wide top of the old stone wall which divided the garden from the orchard. He lay on his back between great tussocks and hanging beards of pinks, staring up into the leaves of a poplar that endlessly moved and murmured together, although only the smallest breeze was stirring. He had been listening a long while, thinking of nothing else at all, until at last it seemed that the voice of the leaves was growing gradually clearer, on the very edge of forming into whispered words, and at the same time he began to have the feeling that someone was watching him. He thought he heard a movement below him, somewhere just behind his shoulder, on the orchard side of the wall, where the water-butt stood. 'Look! Look! Look! There he is!' the leaves seemed to mutter. Nathaniel held his breath a moment, then rolled over suddenly on to his face, to catch whoever it was before he had time to vanish. He was startled to see a dark face directly below, gazing up at him! It was only his own reflection in the water-butt. Yet for a moment it had seemed like someone looking through a window from another world—and surely the face had been smiling? As he turned over, an apple had fallen out of his pocket and dropped with a splash into the water-butt. When the water grew still enough to see once more, the reflection in it was staring darkly up at him with his own puzzled expression. But he was still convinced he had seen it smiling at him, mischievously, when he first moved, wearing just the expression of someone playing Grandmother's Steps, who has stolen up so close to the 'He' that one more step will bring him near enough to pounce, and end the game.

Nathaniel often returned to lean over the water-butt, listening for a warning to grow out of the babble of the poplar leaves, watching for the least sign from the dark image in the water. But nothing more happened.

Then one day in April he was climbing the apple-tree that leant out over the duck-pond, trying to reach what looked like a chaffinch's nest, far out on a lichened branch above the water. He swarmed along the bough, stretching out as far as he dared, but the whole branch leaned under his weight, nearer and nearer to the pond, creaking and cracking dangerously, and the nest was still just beyond his reach and still just above the level of his eyes, so that he could not see into it to count the eggs. He dared not go any further, and was wondering how ever he should get back. He glanced down, and saw in the water a murky, quivering branch with a quivering boy stretched along it. He was convinced he saw the boy's hand, a little ahead of his own, reach out with a quick, light gesture over the rim of the nest, and his lips signal to Nathaniel in delighted triumph the word 'Four!' But in the very instant that he thought he saw this, Nathaniel's grasp had begun to slip, and with a tearing of corduroys he slithered round helplessly under the bough, lost hold with his heels, and dropped disgustedly into two feet of cold April water and soft mud. The bough sprang up out of his hands and a cloud of licheny dust fell into his eyes. He never managed to look into the chaffinch's nest, and after his splashing he could not really be sure whether in his giddiness he had not merely imagined the unlikely behaviour of his reflection. But one curious thing was this. On a warm morning some weeks later, he watched from behind the hedge two anxious chaffinch parents feeding a row of fledglings on the bough above the pond—and sure enough there were four.

One evening in September he dawdled up into the higher garden and sat himself on the edge of the well there, looking down into the water's eye. Because he was bored, and because nothing in the garden offered itself to amuse him, he began to play a private game which he called 'getting into my head'.

It had occurred to him first in the school where he and ten others, all of different ages, did their different lessons round one table. Miss Bone would move from one to the next, pointing out mistakes with a pale, flat finger-tip, and murmuring, 'Before I come back, get *that* into your head.' Nathaniel imagined himself snatching up an armful of the Kings of England and packing them away for ever in a small round upper room, which was his head. 'Exports of Africa', too—such a list to learn—the round room should have a tall cupboard into which he could stuff them pell-mell. But by now he realized he was imagining *himself* inside that room—inside his own head, in fact. After this he could at any time, by concentrating, feel that what was meant by 'I' was not vaguely spread throughout him, arms and legs and all, but gathered up small inside his skull, and looking out through the round windows of his eyes. If Miss Bone were a long while in returning, it could grow very still indeed inside that circular room, with a kind of expectant hush. . . .

This evening the game made him almost afraid, as he sat staring down at his own shadowed face in the water. If he 'got into his head' what might not come into the head of that reflection, which was himself, yet not himself? He sat at his round windows and waited, holding his breath, staring down into the well.

But the thing which then happened did not, at the time, seem strange at all.

Slowly, deliberately, his reflection put a finger to its lips.

Nathaniel's own hands had not stirred from the well-brim. He looked down at the boy in the water, as if from far away, and he felt no surprise. He only thought 'What is he listening to?' Then into that imaginary round room of his head there floated unmistakably the distant sound of water flowing—the sound of a river. It seemed to vary—now nearer, now farther off. It was a kind of whisper, yet with something in it of the sound of bells, so strange that he half-shivered—yet familiar, too, because he had dreamt of it so long. He saw that the boy in the water was smiling, stretching out his hands to him, leaning towards him, up through the water. Nathaniel leant down eagerly to meet him. The noise of the river filled his ears. In a moment more his finger-tips would have touched the other boy's. But from away down the slope of the garden sounded his mother's voice 'Nat! Nat! Na—than—iel!'

Everything else went out of his head. He felt dizzy from stooping, he could not remember what he had been thinking of, and his knees ached from pressing against the wall of the well. It was time to go in, and the garden was growing shadowy. He could not make out the expression on the face in the water. In that circle of reflected dusk, darkening more quickly than the sky above him, a few stars already showed. Yet through his bitter disappointment ran a hope:

'In the morning I shall find my river, and it will be more beautiful than any river in the world.'

TWO

The Secret Valley

But the next morning Nathaniel woke up late, only just in time for breakfast; for rain was falling steadily, dragging down the clouds in ragged scarves till they sank almost on to the tops of the great yews, and the dull glimmer through the window seemed hardly daylight. Nat felt cross and vacant: the day yawned ahead of him with nothing to do in it. There was obviously no chance of finding his river in such a dismally matter-of-fact downpour. He raced raindrops on the window-pane and betted on a fat one that rolled at a smart pace down the glass—but others broke around it so quickly that the racers rolled together into one rivulet and were lost.

Curled up on the window-seat, he watched the thrushes gobbling yew-berries; till Sly, the grey cat, came out down below and they flew off. He dawdled downstairs to tease Sly, who thereupon ran up into the yew-tree in the wet, which he hated, and Nathaniel felt ashamed to see him crouching there with drips falling into his ears. Rough, the rusty-coloured collie, lay spread out flat before the kitchen fire, the curls on his ears in tags of wet felt. He was too bored himself to do more than thump his tail once, and open one eye, when Nat begged him to come out and play.

So Nat spent the day trying to be good, and not succeeding, and the crosser he grew, the more dismally improbable his river became. In the end, he helped Mr. Greenaway, the gardener, to polish the tools in the potting shed, which made him feel better himself, although the river felt as far away as ever.

The truth was, he decided—leaning his chin on his oily hands and staring at the rows of apples stored in the gloom— the truth was that yesterday's sudden enchantment had little to do with being either good *or* bad. It had simply happened, like the wind or the Spring.

He left Mr. Greenaway hissing his endless tune between his yellow teeth, and going back to the house, crowned a long day's dreariness with disgrace. For he filled the bath with cold water to the brim, so that Mr. Greenaway had to stay late and pump a second time. And nobody—not even himself—considered it a good enough excuse that he had wanted to see his own reflection. Yet this day was of a kind he later grew to know well— almost to expect. It never failed to plunge him into gloom, yet a special radiance often seemed to fall on the day that followed.

Next morning he woke very early out of a confusion of happy dreams. The first beam of light slanted across the moss-grown lawn, a thrush was singing 'Be quick! Be quick!' and far down the garden some enormous raindrop blinked yellow and red and green, like a lighthouse furiously signalling.

Nat padded downstairs on stockinged feet. The ashy smell of yesterday's fires hung in the stuffy air, as he slipped past the blue cave of the kitchen whose curtains faced west, and the glowing dusk of the drawing-room whose red curtains had the sun behind them. Not a curtain anywhere was drawn yet and the windows were all locked. The rooms seemed deep in their own private thoughts, as though they had utterly forgotten the human family who lived in them yesterday, and who would come down to claim them again in an hour or two. They gave

Nathaniel a curious feeling, as if either he or they were not quite real. This added zest to his knowledge that just on the other side of their walls all the brilliant, living, singing morning was waiting for him to escape and join it.

He pulled on his boots, pushed open the heavy back door violently, almost as if he were afraid he might be stopped, and as the fresh air stung him into wild excitement, he pelted away through the garden, through the yew-trees where the light fell thin-spun and dusty, down through the woods, plunging and leaping, and never stopped till he reached the shadowy valley.

Once there, he abruptly fell still again, so still was everything about him, serene and drenched, waiting for the sun which began to eat away the edge of the opposite hills. Nathaniel walked in a half-dream, forgetful of himself or why he had come. When his eye fell on a wild flag-pod, open like the jaws of a snake, with orange seeds for teeth, he seemed to know inside him what it meant to lean upon a stem in the damp Autumn air; and when he looked up at faint cries in the sky, and saw a flock of wild duck flying down the valley, he took part in their flight, and felt himself the leader, neck outstretched, the others in a V spread out behind, the sunlight bright and warm already on his whistling wings. It never occurred to him to wonder why duck should be flying over this waterless valley, nor, as he walked, did he wonder why flowers he had never seen before were beginning to carpet the path he trod.

All at once he realized he was in a part of the valley he had never explored before. The ground shelved away ahead. Rustlings and squeakings sounded all about him, wild things crept and hopped close by, and once he heard the long sharp whistle of a bird flying past, as if close by his head, but he saw nothing. As the path grew steeper, these creatures grew bolder; a mouse bundled over his very toes, a red squirrel bent over its branch and threw a nut right into his hair. A moorhen, too, scuttled ahead of him, on black, ungainly legs, tail up over her back, crying 'Fek! Fek!'

'She looks like a hospital nurse in a hurry,' he thought,

'with her black stockings!' He laughed and then pulled up short because he had nearly trodden on a large Roman snail, magnificent in black and yellow stripes, who was labouring slowly across the path. Nat kindly picked him up and put him a little farther on his way, noticing as he did so that the snail did not pull in his horns and disappear in a foamy frill into his shell. On the contrary he was most disinclined to leave, and indeed, when Nat sat down to see what he would do next, he crawled back painfully but with determination on to his boot.

'Very well,' said Nathaniel, '*I* don't object, but I suppose I had better take you the way you were going.'

So he turned off the path where the snail had crossed it, and followed his shadow into the long flowery grass. The snail rode with dignity on the toe of his boot, waving delighted horns in the air. Snails are not, as a race, animals that show their feelings, but this one seemed aquiver with eagerness and would sometimes peer round and up at Nathaniel and then look ahead once more, tremulously, leaning so far out of his shell that it looked as if at any moment it would roll off his back and leave him a mere slug. Nathaniel kept his eyes on him, so he did not see what was ahead of his feet. Without noticing, he climbed a low step of rock and looked down. And there it was, just at his feet—the river!

With a cry he fell upon hands and knees—but remembered not to crush the snail. He set him down, and side by side they craned over the edge of the bank. The water was like crystal. Every weed and speck and stone shone as he had once seen his mother's jewels, when she lost a pearl among them and tipped out the whole boxful tangled together, necklaces and brooches and rings, in the candlelight.

It was quite deep, between its small waterfalls, and more full of bubbles than an ordinary stream, as if it came down with great force from some height. Every stone and filament of root held a long silver bubble bulging and streaming out in the current.

And though it was so narrow here that he could have jumped

across, Nathaniel never doubted it was *the* river, and not a mere
brook or tributary.

'Oh you wonderful snail!' he exclaimed in gratitude, and
began to dance for joy. And the snail, very slowly, began to go
in a circle upon the flat stone. Perhaps if he had been made
differently he would have capered too; but since he was a snail
he crept, and the circle was for pure joy and sympathy.

Nathaniel longed to explore—and yet how could one bear to
leave a place so delicious! It was secret too—that was the best
part of all—entirely his own, for surely not a soul in the world
knew of it. But was he, in fact, quite alone? For as he looked at
his reflection he saw that it was not woodenly mimicking his
gestures, as it had done yesterday. How sulkily it had glowered
back at him out of the depths of that unfortunate bath! But now,
as once before in the well, the figure in the water smiled, waved,
and leant up towards him. Then the boy did something even
more astonishing. He put his hands together as if to dive, and
plunged—not downwards though, but upwards, like a swallow.
The surface broke into rings, and with a scramble up the grassy
bank his reflection was beside Nathaniel and laughing at his
amazement. Nat could think of nothing to say, except: 'But you
haven't got any boots on!' His own feet were warmly stuffed
into gum-boots, but the river boy's toes were bare. This had
caught Nat's eye because his companion was in every other
detail dressed exactly like himself, even to the jagged tear in his
leather jacket which his mother had begun to mend so neatly,
and had finished with long looping stitches because he was
nearly late for school.

'Well,' replied the river boy, 'I couldn't see your feet from
down there—and anyway I prefer bare feet.' Nathaniel had a
moment's pang of jealousy. 'Did you come here before I did?
Do you know the river? I thought perhaps it was undiscovered.'

'I have never really been away from it,' answered the river
boy. 'Only for moments, to run through a mirror. There I am
bound, I must do all that you do. Here I live and play and am
free. I knew you would come one day.'

'But are you just me—or partly me—or someone quite

outside me? Who, exactly, are you?'

'That you will never—exactly—be sure of!' mocked the boy, mimicking him.

'Very well,' said Nat pleasantly, for he took things as he found them and was not persistent. He could always watch, and he was used to finding out what he wanted to know by watching, for most of his companions were animals and birds. Sly would not answer questions about mousing, but he would show Nat how it was done if he sat down patiently by the corn-rick to watch. And the wren whose nest he had once searched for in vain all one long morning, though she had talked a great deal in a sharp voice, did not answer to the point. However, falling silent at last, since the boy had evidently turned into a harmless stump, she ran right under his nose into her round mossy dome among the maze of thick roots.

'Shall we bathe?' Nat suggested, for the Autumn morning was so warm, and how much more fun it would be bathe with this friendly person than by himself, or with grown-ups who insisted he should concentrate on his swimming. Swimming was *not* bathing. Nor was ordinary bathing like this. The boys stripped as they danced about, and plunged into a pool under some overhanging hazel-bushes. The yellow leaves were dropping into water that flowed there over a bed of softest white sand, and sometimes nuts fell in too, with a plop, and the boys cracked and ate them as they floated. The water was mild as warm air, and held them up as if they were mere thistledown. It seemed impossible to sink. They played a dozen games— chasing each other and duck-diving for Nat's old lucky three-penny bit with the hole in it, which shone up brightly against the sand. But it was never quite where he put his hand upon it, and the river boy generally seized it first. Then they climbed the hazel-bushes and somersaulted from them into the pool, or climbing to the quivering tops, bent the whole tree over and slid down headfirst in a rush of yellow leaves.

Tired of this at last, they ran races up and down the bank to get dry, and then flung themselves down in the sun to talk. The river boy told Nathaniel stories—stories he felt he half-knew already; yet the end was always strange to him. Then the boy showed him how to make a minute water-wheel. He fastened pairs of sycamore seeds together, with a pin from a blackthorn. Then, so that it could turn freely, he laid the two ends of the thorn in two hollowed-out pipes of elder, propped on each side by stones, just where the water fell in a toy Niagara. The fans of the sycamore seeds, each set at a slant, just caught the water with their tips and the little wheel began to revolve, slowly at first, then faster and faster, soon spinning too quick for the eye to see. The whole tiny machine was light as a feather and most delicately made. Nathaniel marvelled at the river boy's skill and patience—*that* certainly was no reflection of his own.

They both lay so still, watching the little wheel, that a spider began to attach her thread to Nat's finger and then looped it across to the river boy's shoulder, intending to hang her whole wheel of gossamer between them.

'One day,' said Nathaniel dreamily—for now he had reached the river there seemed all the days of all time in which to enjoy it, and no hurry about anything—'*One* day, shall we explore the river? Which way shall we go? Up to the source or down to the sea?'

'I don't believe you would ever find the source,' said the boy. 'It would be so much farther away than you think.'

'Then let us go to the sea. Do you know the way?'

'Not all of it. That's a long way too, but they say that after-wards it seems to have gone very quickly. Put your ear to the waterfall and you will hear something of what we shall meet on the way.'

Nathaniel lay down, so that the little wheel turned close before his eyes, blotting out the sky; and the cool breath of the falling water brushed his cheek. At first the sound of it was like birds singing and rustling feet, sighings, rushings, whispers. Then more distant and mysterious, with faint shouts and numb silences and a steady roaring like the sound of a weir. Then fiercer, wilder clashings and a soughing of wings; and this altered into a chime of bells ringing as if a whole drowned city's belfries were swaying in the flood. As they faded, these were mixed with the moan of wind in rigging, the rush of foam under a ship's bows. Other sounds he could not name were mingled with all these—voices that spoke to him in a strange language he could almost understand—but never quite: voices calling, inviting, warning, saying farewell. All the while the little wheel spun on, working for nobody. At last, he had listened so long that there was a roaring of blood in his ears which came and went like the sound of waves in a seashell. Surely it was the sea itself? Unimaginably far away, it beat and surged; but faintly, faintly—waves on a strand as far as the world's end.

'Let's go!' he cried. 'Let's start at once!' and sprang to his feet.

But the river boy had stolen away unseen, the little wheel turned no more, the river had vanished like a wreath of mist. This was not even that hidden valley but familiar ground, under the shadow of Bourne Woods, and Nat was fully dressed, and staring at a puddle. The air was chilly and slack, the valley was damp, and it smelt of rotting leaves. He shivered at the bare notion of bathing! From the puddle his own face gazed dumbly and indistinctly back at him. When he stretched out his hand, it stretched out its own. When he frowned, it frowned too. A little maliciously, he stuck out his booted foot over the water. It was exactly reflected, and Nat nodded. 'So there!' He had at any rate put the boy to the trouble of finding his boots.

Then, forgetting crossness in regret, he cried out loud, 'Why, *why* did you have to go away?' And the reflection moved its lips with the same words, whether mockingly or sadly he could not tell. At his feet lay a large Roman snail on a slime-silvered stone. It had described a circle, it seemed, but had not quite completed it. Whether it were *his* snail or no, Nathaniel could not tell, for it had hidden itself completely in its shell and had gone to sleep. There seemed nothing left to do but to go home.

THREE

Hide and Seek

NEXT morning, hardly a thought had come back into Nat's sleep-heavy head before he was stumbling down the hill again, as fast as his legs would go, back to the valley.

But though he tramped it farther than ever before, he found no trace of the river—or of the secret valley. The sunlight seemed feebler, the world somehow smaller than yesterday. The only squirrel he caught sight of jerked its tail at him in timid exasperation, and all the other creatures of the valley skulked out of sight, or flew mutely out of his path, very unlike the friendly ones who had seen him on his way before. As for snails, there were plenty about—too many—*all* crossing the path, and at every angle, and from both sides. Each one he touched shrank at once into its shell, leaving only indignant bubbles at the door. He found no flowers except sodden ragwort and self-heal going brown. And he discovered that he could not even remember the shapes and colours of those which had crowded under his heedless feet, as he lay with the river boy, talking.

At last he gave up searching and sat despondently on a log and brooded, as he had done in the potting shed. What was wrong with the day? Or was something wrong with himself? He went back over yesterday's memories, moment by moment.

'Perhaps,' he wondered, 'it was because I was *not* looking for the river that I found it?' This was not an idea that would have occurred to him before he met the river boy. The Kings of England and the Exports of Africa went in at one ear and out of the other, but the thoughts that grew out of that long murmured conversation, before the little water-wheel had begun to turn—these remained with him and flowed slowly by.

So he got up from his log and stumped home, and was late for breakfast, and late for school, and took his scoldings absent-mindedly, as if that part of life had very little to do with him.

A week or two later—much of it spent in trying hard *not* to look for the river—came that day when Winter takes a sudden leap forward out of the Autumn shadows—the day when the clocks are put back an hour. Next day, instead of a last damp hour with Rough in the gradual October dusk, there was high tea, and Mrs. Dill, the cook, lit a lamp beside the teapot, and the black dark sprang flat up against the window-pane.

Mrs. Dill glided out again on soft flat feet without a word. She was a very thin woman, with large dark eyes and a long straight nose, and when she moved it was all in one, her head never bobbing—like a piece of upright furniture. She wore a perfect Joseph's coat-of-many-colours—clothes that escaped on all sides in wisps, button within buttoned fold. On top of all hung her plain grey apron, behind which her thin hands disappeared as soon as they had laid down whatever they were carrying.

Nat ate his tea more or less by himself; for his mother was busy, as usual, and moved about the room as she ate, leaving oddments of bread and butter perched on corners of mantelpieces and window-sills, till she should think of them again; and Grandfather dozed off between one cup of tea and the next.

By the time Nat had finished, Mrs. Dill had glided in again to draw the curtains. Nat was disinclined to amuse himself—not yet reconciled to this new stretch of indoor time, with its books and draughts and dominoes. He was accustomed to staying out from the bells of four o'clock, that ended school, till his bedtime. He would often take his tea with him to eat on the brick wall of the garden, still warm from the sun, with a Sly and a Rough unusually full of affection as they both watched his disappearing hunk of lardy-cake, one from each side. So now he slipped out after Mrs. Dill and asked her to play hide and seek with him, while she locked up and shut the shutters all over the house. She never hid—though she would have fitted excellently into a number of thin, shadowy corners, between tallboys and grandfather clocks, for instance. But she was unfailingly astonished whenever she found him. As they worked their way towards the top of the house, Nat fled away before her up into his own attic. This had a private stair, as well as a cupboard in the wall that stretched so far along into the roof that it was in itself almost a second, secret room. The attic had an entrance like a burrow, an irregular plaster tunnel about four feet long. Inside, the room slanted up on all sides, more like a rabbit's nest than ever, with a very low, many-angled ceiling, almost domed, and a number of joists poking through here and there at random, as though they were part of the great roots of a tree above. On the floor by the bed was a sheep-skin. Nat kept all he cared about in a big black box, which was very heavy and curiously fitted up with wooden chocks inside, for it had once held part of a ship's gun. Everything he did *not* care about—his clothes in fact—was bundled into a squat brown chest of drawers, from which socks and braces and ties hung out like panting tongues. On top of this were some tattered books, a bundle of bracken Nat was drying for tobacco, a blue speckled china cow, and a crystal ball on a black wooden stand.

Outside the small dormer window, ivy thrust up a thick head of stalks over the gutter right on to the tiles, and housed all the sparrows of Bourne. The wall here was a good yard thick, so that the sill made a comfortable seat: that is, if you measured not more than two feet long when folded double. Drawing the curtain behind him now, Nat sat clasping his knees and looked out over slate roofs, glimmering in the strengthening moonlight

—away to the hill-top copse. A pair of chimney cowls, on the roof whose ridge ran at right angles to his room, stood up together on one stack, pitch black against the faintly-lit sky. They looked, at night, like two people with their arms linked, and because they had round cowls that spun in the wind—one fast, one slowly and unwillingly—there was always a movement, a suggestion of life about their heads, as though they breathed and perhaps talked, or were counting stars while they looked up. Farther away still, the stable, no longer used, humped its thatched roof all in black; and at the end of the higher garden sailed the derelict dovecote, all in white, already blanched by the moon.

Mrs. Dill never came. She had forgotten all about Nathaniel. It did not matter; for he was no longer waiting for her. He had forgotten everything but the transformation of the garden as it stole, bush by bush, into light. This was a brighter moonlight than he ever remembered, with something of gold in it, like sunlight mixed with night. The sparrows in the ivy-covered gutter were behaving in an unusual way. He was used to their occasional tiffs at night, and the muffled cheep from a beak tucked under a small, stuffy wing. But tonight, from the whole length of the gutter came a restless churring and chattering, like a dormitory of boys at a midnight feast.

Far off in her high sloping meadow, he could see that Old Rose, his mother's pony, was also restless. He heard her hooves click against the stones as she roved up and down, stopping now and then with head upflung towards the crest where the moon would soon appear. He could see her cloudily glimmering, even among the dark trees; for in her extreme old age (she had lived at Bourne for thirty years) all the dapples of her coat and her dark mane and tail had faded white.

It was long since anyone had ridden her, but Nathaniel had looked out of nursery and attic window to see her ghosting past on the green hill, every day of his life. She would mumble a lump of sugar from his hand till she had dyed it green with grass-juice, and then drop it, and lose it, and nod drowsily to say she had been grateful for the brief pleasure. Sometimes on a very wild moonlight night, or when a distant hunting-horn sounded, she would forget her old age and career across her field, snorting and arching her neck. But this last year she had grown more thin and bowed than ever, and her eyes were sunk deep in their sockets. Instead of fattening on the Summer grass, she grew thinner even than in the Winter, and her teeth were almost all gone. What most distressed Nathaniel and his mother —for they loved her dearly—was that magpies and crows had lately taken to perching on her back and riding there, while she cropped or stood, half-asleep, drooping upon three legs, resting one. The birds seemed to realize how near to death she was, and treated her as if she were already only a lump of earth.

The moon was creeping up behind the two watching chimneys; already its gleaming rim was eating into their cowls. A moment after, streaming over the edge, its enormous light blazed full into Nathaniel's eyes. He gazed and gazed, as the whole round of it gradually swam clear—so brilliant that all the mountains and dead seas on its face were hidden in their own radiance. At last he could bear it no longer and lowered his dazzled eyes. Red and green circles danced giddily in front of them wherever he looked. Before his sight had quite cleared again, he noticed that Old Rose, now white as a bone in the full light, was stooping her head to the drinking-trough. As she did so he leant forward to see her better, and the broad, bright reflection of the moon slid into the water just under her nose. He saw her drink, and it was as if she were drinking the moon itself. The ripples spread in wildly flashing rings, wider and wider, till they seemed to overflow the trough and circle round Old Rose herself—and at that moment she vanished. Nathaniel looked about for her, but the field was empty, sloping in silver and black down to the silent woods. He looked back at the reflection of the moon in the trough, still shaking to and fro, and suddenly it looked to him like an unlatched door, a round silver door, idly swinging. Just then a gust shook down a swarm of elm-leaves over the roof behind his head, whirling down to meet their reflections in the puddles along the path. In falling past the window they touched Nathaniel's brow and hair and hand as if inviting him to join them. Lightness and excitement filled him—he too had slipped loose from the life that tied him by the stalk, he too would go. There was the round silver door of the moon's reflection, still swinging in the dark water. In another instant he was through it, and the world of Bourne vanished as if the moon had driven it like a shadow from before her face.

FOUR

The Forest Dancing

HE came to himself, kneeling in a bed of fern at the edge of a
forest—a forest that had felt no breath of Autumn, for it smelt
of early Summer flowers. At his feet shone the wavering face of
the same full moon, however, but reflected this time not in the
still water of Old Rose's trough, but in the river—running deep
and very swiftly, full to the brink. And yet—and yet, had there
been nothing in between? Had he not travelled in some way he
could not remember, those many miles which must lie along the
banks between that early morning bathing-place of his first
visit, where the young river had been no bigger than a brook,
and these smooth, midnight reaches? If he had indeed walked
beside the river in his dreams, he could recall nothing now of
the countryside through which he had passed. Yet sometimes in
a vacant hour at school, or while his mother had played to him

on the piano, or at the very first instant of waking, he had come to himself with a start to find something altered, as though he did not stand quite where he had stood a minute before. Had he been travelling then, even while he had seemed to be away? He gave up puzzling—enough that Old Rose had opened the way back for him again; enough that he was here, with the whole mysterious night to enjoy.

The silver-gold moonlight so flooded the air, it seemed he must be breathing light, almost drinking it; he half-believed that if he launched out on his arms into it, the brightness would bear him up, and let him swim upon it. His outstretched hands, sleeved in black shadow to the wrist, shone so white they seemed to belong to somebody else; the blood itself felt like quicksilver through all his body. Nothing stirred under the light except the rushing river. The fresh dark skirts of the trees, drenched in dew, brooded motionless, tip to tip with their dark reflections. On the ground every rib and freckle on every fallen leaf stood out stark and clear and still as marble. Nathaniel, caught by the spell of quietness, stared so long at the river that when at last he looked up, the whole strange world of night seemed to be drifting the other way, as if the river stood still and the solid earth flowed upstream.

While he still knelt bemused, he began to hear the music.

At first he thought it was just fancy; then that it must be the blood roaring in his ears, from hanging his head down so long. But as he stood up to listen better, his shadow stole out black before him, and he saw—lying in it with his hands behind his head—the river boy. And he could see that he was listening too. They did not speak, but only looked wonderingly at one another, because now the sound welled out across the leagues of dark tree-tops: a silvery piping, mounting higher and higher; then dying away down so deep, it seemed to hum underground, as if it were the earth itself humming, spinning itself to sleep like a huge top.

The sound was not only beautiful: it had a power that made Nathaniel shiver. For without his will or wish, his feet had begun to move towards it. It was calling him away and he felt he could not choose, but must follow wherever it led.

But the river boy raised his hand and Nathaniel stopped to look up where he was pointing, into the oak-tree overhead. The lowest boughs, outspread flat, were so ribbed and broad and ancient that thick gardens of ferns and mosses had grown along them, and among these Nathaniel made out, by the glint of its eye in the moonlight, the shape of a small bird moving. It was putting its head first to one side, then the other, and leaning its breast against the bark and half-spreading its wings, as if it were listening intently too. Then as though it could contain itself no longer, it cocked its tail over its back like a wren and burst into song, so loudly Nat's ears rang. First a cascade of notes poured down; then his own joy seemed to choke the singer, and only thick, slurring cries would come. 'Jug! Jug! Jug!' he shouted, till his voice cleared again and floated out in long pure notes like a flute: 'Tereu! Tereu! Tereu!'

'Oh, it must be a nightingale!' whispered Nat excitedly, for he had never heard one at Bourne, however long he lay awake on late Spring nights.

The wonderful voice of the bird had distracted him for a moment; but now, as it fell silent, the other, mysterious music stole out again, all the more distant, shivery and uncanny after that warm, excited song. The nightingale seemed to be drawn by it, as Nathaniel was; it flew downstream and perched in a thick hawthorn over the water and sang again, and then flew on, farther and farther, as if it could not bear to follow without singing in reply, but feared to sit and sing too long in case the music should move away altogether without it.

The spell of stillness had been broken. Everything that had been waiting, stock-still, was now astir and awake. The trees sighed and moved their branches restlessly, bringing down the dew in pattering showers. Owls hooted to and fro across the river, and small creatures in the undergrowth scuttered and rustled and thumped out signals across the deep, soft floor of leaf-mould.

And with the bursts and dying falls of that music which had roused them, another music rose all around—a mist of faint, small, earthly voices, chirruping, twittering, trilling, as if it were daybreak, instead of full moon and midnight. Surely that was a thrush! And nearer, a robin. And now a wren—bursting out like a little crystal bottle suddenly unstoppered! It was extraordinary in the solemn silver light to hear all the small birds of day singing until the air seemed to tingle, and that other uncanny piping threaded in and out among them, almost smothered by them all. 'But it's not the birds themselves,' murmured Nathaniel, half to himself, half to the river boy. 'This is what makes them sing, but it isn't birdsong. They're only listening, like us, and following.'

'Yes,' replied the river boy.'All their singing is only answering.'

'I *wish* I could sing,' sighed Nathaniel. 'Let's follow, it's moving farther off.'

Because the strangeness of the sound over-awed them both, they took each other by the hand as they pushed through the leaves into the sweet-scented darkness under the trees, keeping as near as they could to the friendly, guiding river, exactly above whose course a faint road of starlit sky wound to and fro, narrowing but not lost even where the trees leaned most thickly together.

Soon Nathaniel began to notice a curious thing. Whenever he stood still to listen, the music faded. But if he happened to glance at the river boy, whom nothing could sober for long, jigging about softly or swinging from a low branch, the music revived again, as if it were shaken out of silence by his dancing feet or the flickering of his sleeve. So Nathaniel began to hop about a little himself, and found that when he did so, the tune grew livelier and plainer. So their hushed, timid advance, stealing through the trees hand in hand, became by degrees a dance instead—wilder and bolder as they went on, in and out of dazzling shafts of light and deep pools of shade, or criss-cross dizzy stripes of both. Round and round some huge hollow trunk they would whirl, till the night spun round them—then they would break apart and speed down separate glades, and when they met again and paused for breath, silence came down close about them like a softly folding cloak. As soon as they could, they would set off again, for the sheer delight of hearing the piping once more climb to the stars and throb round them, loud and sweet.

They were not the only travellers on foot that night. Several times Nat thought he heard twigs snapping, and a thud, thud, like a pony's hooves, trotting steadily, always just out of sight ahead. Once they tumbled out of a thicket upon a strange and lovely sight—in a little open clearing round which the river circled, holding back the trees with its silver arm, there were seven deer. The boys stopped short, in time to sink into the bracken unobserved, where they peered through the stems. There were four shadowy does at the edge of the clearing, milling about together, sliding their chins along each other's soft backs, dancing on legs as thin as reeds, stamping and backing and advancing. In the middle of the open stage two majestic stags were side-stepping opposite one another, very stately and slow. Their wide-spread antlers clashed as they bowed their heads together, locked horns and swung from side to side. Then they would break apart and rear up and up on their hind legs, till they looked like two dancing trees, with heads of branches, bowing to the moon. And all this while, underneath the bellies of the does, so small and so silent Nathaniel did not notice him at first, a little fawn was intent upon his own private dance, to a rhythm twice as fast as all the others. In and out of the flashing legs he leapt and pirouetted, with his gliding shadow on the ground for partner, and he took no notice of anybody else. Nathaniel could have lain there for ever, watching that wild seven bruise with their sharp hooves a green circle in the grass, elsewhere all as white as salt with moonlit dew. But without warning, when the dance was at its wildest—suddenly they were all gone, all in one bound, one crash through the wet leaves—like water flung out of a bowl with a splash. The music drifted farther off, accompanied by its cloud of darkling birdsong—no doubt the deer would follow it to the next dancing-floor, and there begin afresh. But Nathaniel longed to have touched the fawn, to have held it for just one moment, warm and breathing in his arms.

After they had disappeared, but while he still lay with his

chin in the moss under the bracken, he realized that all this while another dance had been going on under his nose, unnoticed. In their forest of the bracken a little company of ants were weaving in and out, circling and exchanging partners, and in a corner, under the fronds of moss, mites even tinier, specks of life hardly visible even in the brilliant light, were moving mazily on the floor of their own miniature woodland which towered inch-high above their heads.

When he rolled on his back he saw the pulsing stars divide before the slow-paced moon, and a shooting star spring out across her path. He thrust his hand with all his force against the tree-trunk by his head, and thought he could feel, through bark and all, the faint thrilling of the sap. He imagined it as an invisible green fountain, playing to the music, inside the wooden body of the tree, springing higher and higher through all its branches, spraying out into every topmost twig and leaf. He became aware that the dancing was going on all around him, in everything he could see—and who could tell what singing there was too?—music too faint, or too high, or too low for human ears to catch, but going on all the same.

The river boy was turning cartwheels, a star of white legs and arms flashing stiffly and slowly, in and out the thin wheel of shadows under a pine-tree. Nathaniel ran to him suddenly and caught him by the feet to make him stop and attend, so that the boy looked comically up at him, upside down, his face shadowy, as if it were once more only a face in water.

'Oh, listen! listen!' cried Nathaniel, as the music pierced through him: 'How can you *bear* to stay playing here when it's still so far off? We must find it! Don't you *care* whether you reach it or not?'

The boy kicked his legs free and lay there smiling. 'No I don't. I love all this—the fine night, and the forest and the dancing. I just want to dance. Isn't it enough for you?'

'No, it isn't! It isn't!' exclaimed Nat. He had never felt the difference between them so much before. He longed to make the river boy understand, and feel as he felt.

'Oh, don't you see? Haven't you ever felt—this isn't the only time—I've felt it at Bourne sometimes—as if you suddenly almost *understand*—understand *everything* I mean—what the wind means in the trees, what the river's saying—*everything*? And if only we could get there, to the music, I think I should *quite* understand this time. I'm sure of it.'

'And why the birds sing?' asked the boy softly. But Nathaniel saw he was on the edge of teasing.

Then the boy went on: 'No, I don't feel like that. I feel like *them*—like the trees and the birds. Leaves or feathers, or hands and feet, or shadows and reflections—it makes no difference which you have. Everyone must sing and dance as best he can! But I don't want to know *why*. Why should I?'

He sprang up and began jigging down the path the deer had made, snapping his fingers and clicking his heels, and, to Nathaniel's exasperation—for he could not echo a phrase of it himself—humming the melody of the music that they heard. Nathaniel felt he could not bear it much longer, if he could neither answer the music with music of his own, nor catch up with it. He rushed after the river boy, and linking arms, they sped together down a long slope, half dancing, half tussling, till the forest rocked about them and their breath was gone.

FIVE

The Water Garden and
the Music-Maker

THEY made a great noise in their headlong descent; for the path grew steeper and twistier, and they loosened great stones that came bounding down behind them, and sent the boys plunging on more recklessly than ever, to escape being hit. They had no time to notice anything ahead, until Nathaniel thought he saw a spark flash out, and then another, in the dimness below. He pulled up, panting, to watch for it again, and this time, unmistakably, a horse-shoe rang out on a stone and a pale form showed against the rocks.

'Why, I believe it's Old Rose! We've found her! Oh, Rose! Rose! Wait for me!'

But the old pony had disappeared again round the next corner and the boys began to notice a dull, gentle roaring below them, a trembling of the rocks underfoot, and a trembling too of the cool air which eddied up round their hot faces, and smelt of fountain-spray.

As they rounded the corner, the sound grew suddenly louder,

pouring and tinkling, almost under their feet, it seemed. The moon was sinking, and her light grew softer in a sky where a faint green line began to finger the horizon. Directly below them the boys saw a great bowl of gaunt, fantastic rocks, over which the forest trees hung on every side. From all round the jagged mossy lips of this huge arena, water was falling into its depths. The river that had flowed, for the last miles, almost invisibly under briars and ferns, now broke out into the open, running round the crater and pouring out from under rocks and under roots, to descend the walls of the pit in sheets and curtains and ropes and glimmering spray.

Whatever lay at the bottom was hidden entirely by something which seemed to be a great shallow white dome or shell. Smooth and dazzling as snow, it roofed the pit from side to side, a little way below the brink. The sound of the water falling rang up from underneath it, with a strange, muffled echo. And the music—the wild music that had enticed them to this place, mingled with the rushing echo. But now it was no longer a wandering sound. It rose up steadily, close at hand at last. This, surely, was its secret home.

Others seemed to think so too; for the dark trees, which stood out sharply against that green light stealing over the eastern rim, were alive with all the birds of the forest that had followed the piping throughout the night and gathered there. They were not singing now, but first one and then another would dart down and flutter just above the white roof, as if frantically seeking a way in, and then, as suddenly, rise in alarm and return to the sheltering leaves.

'Come! Come! Come!' The music seemed to throb with invitation, softlier now, but more persuasively than ever. 'The night is ending!' it seemed to sing. 'Come and rest, traveller, come and rest!'

And up from under the white roof came faintly a long, wild neighing.

At that Nathaniel began to run, seized, he knew not why, by alarm. He must get to Rose, darling Rose, before anything happened. He did not know what it was he feared for her, only

that the sweet invitation, 'Come and rest!', filled him with sad-
ness and foreboding. He felt it called him to say farewell, before
it was too late, to something he had always loved.

He reached the end of the path at the brink of the rock-face,
and could not imagine how Old Rose had gone down. But if she
had, then he could follow! He grasped a thick twist of honeysuckle that hung down to the white dome, and lowered himself
over the edge backwards, feeling with his toes for the top of the
mysterious roof. But he slithered farther and farther, meeting no
firm foothold, and looking down, saw in panic that what he had
taken for a solid roof was only thick mist, into which he already
dangled up to the waist. He tried to scramble up again, but the
honeysuckle tangle unravelled in his hands and let him down,
loop by loop, into the blinding ghostly whiteness, slipping and
dropping until suddenly he fell outright, with tight shut eyes,
through the watery air, to land heavily in thick moss, unhurt.
An instant later the river boy was beside him.

They scrambled to their feet and looked about them. Some
way above, overhead, spread the underside of the curved,
luminous roof, through which enough mother-of-pearl light
floated down to show them they were in an ancient sunken
garden, walled about with falling water, a garden whose
flowers were continually nodding and dancing in the shaken air.
Nathaniel had never seen such flowers, all tumbled together in
a lovely neglect—tall lilies in leaning sheaves, and dark masses
of roses bowed over to the ground, but all turning their thousand
faces up to his, as if to ask, 'Who are you? And why have you
come among us?' The floor of the garden seemed partly of
earth, partly of moving water, but it was hard, in the uncertain
light, to be sure where one ended and the other began. Here a
terraced lawn seemed to spread, but great water-lilies were
strewn across it; and there a dark pool fringed with ferns turned
out to be only a circle of velvet moss. Apple-trees and weeping
willows stood with their feet in running streams, and white
currants hung like strings of water-drops out of the very middle
of a small cascade.

The sliding walls of water—the dancing trembling flowers—

the music that rose from the ground underfoot and flew and fluttered, echoing from rock to rock—made Nathaniel's head swim, after his great fall. He picked his way giddily across to where he saw, with relief, Old Rose waiting for him at last. Her sides were heaving, and flecks of foam splashed her neck. She seemed worn out with her wandering and her impatience. For still she tossed her head, and listened, and moved restlessly, pawing the earth as if she were waiting at a door to be let in.

'Oh, Rose, don't go any farther, rest here!' Nat begged, and offered her handfuls of rushes to eat, and led her to the pools to drink. He longed to lie down himself, and sleep in this hidden place, so full of fruit and flowers. Several times, at Bourne, when he had found a particularly secret spot, he had built himself a house there—some little tumbledown cabin of dead bracken, or hut of twigs and moss—where he could crouch, forgotten by the wild things, and watch what went on in the places where no man ever came. So now he thought of building one here, a house where they could all rest after the journey, with a stall for Old Rose. Sleep was heavy on him, but if he lay down on the soft moss and listened to the lullaby of the water-music, he might sleep so deep that Rose would be gone before he woke, and he might never find her again. As a matter of fact, there seemed to be no way out at all, for the walls of water rose shimmering on every side. However, Old Rose would not be satisfied; she was still roving to and fro, hunting for a way. If they built her a stall, they could tether her and sleep in peace.

So he and the river boy built a cabin together, between the stems of a group of willows, with a pool of flowering irises at the door—a house of apple branches, bound together with vines of traveller's joy. The floor was of moss, and an archway led through into a stall for Old Rose, where Nathaniel heaped up the rushes and ferns for her bed. They worked without speaking much, lost in a drowsy dream. It was strange to see the rose-colour of day-break stealing across that low, blind sky of mist— strange, when they were hungry, to put a hand into the water-falls and pick a bunch of green grapes from under the bubbles— strange to rest from work a moment, in the shadows of the leaf-smelling house, and feel it vibrate around them, as if they were inside a violin that some great hand was playing.

At last the roof was finished, and Nathaniel led Old Rose gently inside and put her in the stall, and fastened a barrier of branches, as strong as he could make it, across the doorway. Then he and the river boy went off to gather fruit for a meal before they slept, and as they left they heard Old Rose pawing the earth in her stall and whinnying. They were not gone long, and came back with their arms full of fruit. As they wound between the mounds of roses, the low misty dome began to flush and glow with gold, and under it the little house of green branches twangled and throbbed, and seemed to cry more clearly than everything else in the echoing garden: 'Come in and rest!'

Nathaniel hurried to the door in joy—but as he crossed the threshold all the fruit fell from his arms and rolled unheeded across the floor. The barrier was unbroken, but Old Rose's stall was empty!

By the heap of rushes he had put for her bed, a dark hole had opened into the earth. Shallow, crumbling, earthy steps led down out of sight. And down the steps, under the garden, the music pulled Nathaniel by the feet. He looked back once at the restful green room they had built, and at the picture of the garden, glittering and dazzling now, as sunrise streamed brilliantly through the low golden sky, all framed in the leafy shadows of the door. How he had longed to stay, to watch the day out in that garden—to explore all its enchanted ground, and learn the music underfoot until he could sing it himself— or hollow out a pipe and play it.

He turned back with a sigh to the dark stairway. Perhaps he would be able to coax Old Rose back up those steps again; but in his heart he knew he would not. Step by step he went down into darkness, until he came out at last on a ledge, facing a narrow gulf, with a great waterfall in it, that fell from the gloom overhead and vanished somewhere far below his feet. He could not see what was above him. The air was fresh and cool. Yet he felt certain he was right underneath the garden, and that all the waters of his river were in this cascade. He felt sure they had sunk through the earth of the garden and were gathering together here to continue once more on their way towards the sea. Now the music echoed as though in a hollow chamber, and it was so loud and sweet, even above the roar of the fall, that it filled Nathaniel's ears, and made it hard for him to think of anything else. A faint light, green and crystal-clear, seemed to pour down from the water itself—or from what lay behind the fall. For Nathaniel began to see, as his eyes and ears grew accustomed to the roaring gloom, that the water fell sheer across the face of a little grotto, set back, just opposite him, behind the curtain of spray. And gradually he began to see, too, on the back wall of this grotto, the indistinct outlines of some ancient carving.

He leant out over the narrow gulf as far as he dared, and looked through the waterfall as though it were a great glass window. Presently he realized that the carving was of an immense face: the gravest, strangest face he had ever seen. It was more like a woman's than a man's, although it was bearded. The eyes were huge and slanting, and stared blindly back at him. Long curling locks spread back from that dark brow and lost themselves in the rocks of the grotto wall. Difficult as it was to see through the shifting pane of water, what with the darkness, and the mosses that half-concealed the great features, Nathaniel could make out that it was the face of someone intently hearkening—some being who had listened through endless ages to the self-same music that had led him here. Then he saw that this listener was not only listening. He was also the maker of the music, or at least its guardian. For just below the dark, half-parted lips an indistinct hand held up a set of stone pipes, almost hidden in weeds. The water of the fall, endlessly altering its flow, splashed over them and through them—now fast, now slow. It was the river that played in them, instead ot breath. And from those crumbling pipes all that magic music came.

For a long while Nathaniel stood motionless, trying to read the secret of those sightless eyes; and in a half-dream, without surprise, he saw that by the music-maker stood a narrow door, fast shut, cut in the solid rock at the back of the grotto.

He did not hear Old Rose step out of the shadows behind him until she stood beside him. He only turned and saw her as she gathered her feet under her for a leap. Her eyes were fixed on the waterfall, and seemed to burn with longing.

Then he flung himself on her, to hold her back, but it was too late. She shook him off like a water-drop, and sprang full at the curtain of water, and passed through it, and landed in the dry grotto inside, and the waters closed behind her.

As she stood there, already veiled by the waterfall and indistinct, Nathaniel heard the music-maker begin a new tune for her. The pipes no longer played 'Come and rest!' but 'Come and dance!' The tune was as gay as the melody that Nathaniel and the river boy had frolicked to in the forest, but stranger and more lovely; and as it struck up, the little door began to move inward upon its hinge.

For a moment Nathaniel caught, through it, a glimpse of some unimaginable country, folded in a dazzling deep blue darkness. Then Old Rose, with a whinny of joy, had passed through, and the narrow door was softly closing. The music faded away, and though the waterfall still roared, it seemed to Nathaniel that a great unbearable silence had fallen on all things.

He did not want to bring Old Rose back now—only to be there himself, in the land that lay under his river—in the opposite direction to his own journey—through the narrow door that was still not quite shut. Nowhere but there would he ever hear again the music of the dance to which she had been called.

He heard the river boy cry out behind him: 'Not yet! Not yet! Come back! It's not time for you yet!' He felt him grip his arm. Like Rose he shook himself free; and like Rose he leapt. But his spring fell short, and he never set foot in the grotto. He saw the door shut in the instant that the torrent caught him and carried him down.

The waters of his river seized him and bore him away, they rolled over his head like sleep, and he fell into deep sleep like a stone.

* * * * *

When his mother came to tell him it was long past bedtime, she found him fast asleep on his window-sill, and so she undressed him herself. He hardly roused, even when she pulled the clothes over his head, so she put him in between the sheets as softly as she could and tiptoed out without a word.

In the morning she had to break the news to him that Old Rose had died the evening before. Probably in her sleep, she said. It was the first time Nathaniel had had to face the death of anyone he loved dearly; yet his mother was puzzled, so little did he say. It was almost as if he knew already. Presently she saw him sitting on the meadow bank, his arm round Rough, staring down into the drinking-trough, and she wondered what they were thinking of, sitting there so still.

SIX

The Earthen Lamp

NATHANIEL's visits to the river were sometimes long ones, when he spent a whole day playing and exploring with the river boy— always farther and farther downstream. But sometimes they were so short that he was there and back between the tick and the tock of the grandfather clock, or between a question of his mother's and his own reply—for she never expected a very quick answer from him. Once, in the depths of Winter, he was sitting curled up on Grandfather's knee, staring into the fire in the high, dark little smoking-room that the ash-tree was always trying to get into—thrusting its knobby grey fingers up against the window-panes. The fire smoked; the ash-tree creaked; draughts squinnied into the room through every cranny: Grandfather was asleep, and nothing could have been more comfortless and solitary. Suddenly, glancing up, he caught a glint, in

Grandfather's spectacles, which had slipped to the end of his nose—not of firelight, but of the sparkle of a silver ripple. Quietly, just behind him, he heard the river boy say: 'Look!'

Turning, startled, Nat saw the river twinkling in an early Summer noon. Close to his nose a big mayfly, just out of its sheath, was drying its wings in the sun. Presently it swung out into the air, and began to dance, springing up higher and higher, and sinking slowly, balancing with its long forked tail. Then it sank too low—brushed the surface of the water. Up flew a pointed shadow from beneath: a little fish flashed into the air, snapped his jaws, and was gone again under the green ripple with the mayfly. But barely had it sunk an inch before a scream-ing whistle sounded over Nathaniel's head, and the loveliest bird he had ever seen shot down into the water after the fish. It was a kingfisher, gleaming blue and green. It flew under the water and was out again in an instant with its prey. Perching on a twig near Nathaniel's face, it gave the fish one fillip to twist it end-on in the great beak, instead of sideways; whistled once again, just to show it *could* with its mouth full; swallowed the fish, and was off. The sparkles of the water turned into a shower of sparks up the chimney, and all was gone. Nathaniel sat blinking his eyes, quite breathless at the speed of it all. Grand-father growled: 'Well, whatever was *that* all about?'

Nat looked at him suspiciously. Had he seen anything? 'Why, you were asleep, Grandfather!' he said firmly.

'Fiddle!' said Grandfather. '*You* were asleep and jumping about in my arms like—like a little trout!' So Nathaniel left it at that, and did not argue. Enough for him to have been by the river for a moment, to have seen its waters shining, felt the sunlit wind on his head; to know it was still there, close by the edge of ordinary life.

Winter wore away into early Spring, the frosts and sodden rains were over, the earth began to smell delicious again. Nathaniel even enjoyed digging it, and went to help Mr. Greenaway one afternoon in the higher garden.

While he was uprooting a truant foxglove by the well, Nat

chanced on a pocket of real blue-grey clay. He dug out a lump
and moistened it in a cloth bag and began to model. He tried
to make a kingfisher, perched on a branch with a fish in his beak.
But it was too dumpy, and the beak, whatever he did to it,
looked clumsy instead of powerful, and it bent at the end with
its own weight. So he pressed with his thumbs a big hollow in
the middle of its back, and curved the beak right round into a
handle, and made himself a clay lamp like a Roman's. He baked
it in the oven very slowly, with Mrs. Dill hovering despondently
in the background. In spite of her mournful prophecies ('It will
crack, I said it will crack and fall into my nice rice-pudding!')
it did not crack, but turned red with black patches and baked
as hard as stone. Nat collected every bit of candlegrease he
could find, every drip, every flat coin of grease left at the bottom
of candlesticks. He even cheated by opening the drawing-room
window and door, so that the tall red candles on the mantel-
piece guttered in the draught and wove long shrouds all down
one side. All these pieces he put in his lamp. Then he went out
to find a rush in the orchard ditch and peeled it and plaited the
pith, and stuck it in the middle for a wick. By the time he had
quite finished, it was growing dusky—the very clear soft dusk of
Spring. Nathaniel took his lamp out of doors and stood it on the
roots of the ash-tree to light it for the first time. The roots
formed a kind of table on the top of the bank. At first the flame
bunched up small and bluish on the pith wick; but as the wax
melted and the wick warmed up and began to float, the flame
climbed higher. It flickered and flapped, throwing a smoky
flare, much brighter than a candle-flame, over the gigantic
roots of the ash, even lighting up the great looping branches
overhead, which were breaking into tufts of flower. Its light
made the dusk deeper and bluer; a primrose close by, growing
in a hole in the roots, shone out strangely and threw its jigging
shadow upward.

Nathaniel was delighted. He so seldom managed to make
anything that really worked, or turned out at all as he had
imagined it. He picked up the lamp and, sheltering the flame
with his hand, began to walk to the house, to show his mother.

In his path, under the ash-tree, was a big puddle. Not looking where he was going, he stepped on to the edge of it. Just as a hoop stands up if you tread on its rim, so, as Nathaniel stood on the edge of the puddle, it sprang up all round him like a hooped frame, and he walked straight through it—to meet the river boy face to face, also sheltering a lamp-flame and not looking where he was going!

They bumped into each other, and both laughed and said at the same moment, 'Clumsy! Look what I've got!' The lamps were not exactly alike. The river boy's was just what Nat had planned and designed but could not quite make. It was finer and smoother, without any burnt patches, and all over its surface were delicate patterns, made by pressing the skeletons of leaves into the clay while it was still damp. Nathaniel had tried this out rather unsuccessfully and smearily.

'Yours is *so* much better than mine,' he said sadly.

'Ah, but you made yours first,' said the boy, smiling. 'I watched you. And anyway it doesn't matter which of us made which. It all comes to the same in the end.'

'I suppose so,' said Nat. 'If you are me and I am you, but I'm never so sure of *that*. And what is all this on your sleeve?' He made a dash at the boy and brushed his sleeve, and a cloud of white powder flew up.

'Why, it's flour!' he exclaimed, examining a pinch in the lamplight. 'Where *have* you been? I've seen it on your clothes before. I saw it all over your collar the day you called me to look at the kingfisher.'

'Ah yes, I had taken an hour off that day—*wasn't* it a hot day!'

'Wasn't it a cold, draughty, rainy, smoky day, you mean! It was in *our* part of the world,' retorted Nat. 'And what do you mean by an hour off? An hour off *what*?'

'Well, now you have noticed the flour, I suppose I had better take you there,' said the river boy, mischievously vague. 'Come on then, I will take you to supper with him.'

'Come on *where*?—and supper with WHOM?' But the river boy was already vanishing over the hedge with his lamp in his hand.

'Bring a light to light you there!' he mocked; and disappeared.

Nat scrambled after him more slowly, guarding his flame.

On the other side of the bank was a path running close along the river-bank. Green, open fields stretched away beyond the river, with only small hills and hollows, to the mountains. These were never out of sight, and bordered the countryside of the river along all its length. The clear evening hung in the air as if it would never deepen into night. Far down the path, Nathaniel saw the other light twinkling as the river boy padded along on bare feet. He took off his own sandals and tied their straps together and slung them through his belt, and then set off running to catch up. The Spring earth and moss were delicious underfoot. His mother had forbidden him to go barefoot so early in the year, but that could only apply to the ordinary world—nobody, surely, could catch cold here.

As he ran, it seemed to him that the light in the air, the green fields, and even the small weeds and scraps of twig and root on which he trod—all held the peculiar still gloss of things reflected in water. And every little hill, though new to him as he passed it, had something in its shape which reminded him of home. Yet they were not like the hills of Bourne, and he could not remember ever having lived anywhere else. As often happened, questions began to gather in his mind like clouds, but whenever he was just on the point of putting them into words, the river boy would turn his smiling face, and Nat would forget all about them—until the next time.

'We must take the Miller a present,' said the boy. 'He loves anything odd, or rare, or out of season.'

'Is it this Miller we are going to supper with?' asked Nat.

'Yes.'

'Who is he?' But Nathaniel might just as well have saved his breath; for the river boy would never, never say who anybody was. Like a signal, the moment the question was out of Nat's mouth, a shrill whistle sounded upstream, and by flew the kingfisher, close over the water, turning first on one wing, then on the other, now burning blue, now green.

'He'll be there before us!' cried the boy, and began to hurry.

Nat jogged alongside in companionable silence, looking after his lamp. Tiny white moths kept blowing up like ashes from underfoot, and they *would* fly into the flame, breaking their silence with a sharp 'Frtt!' as they were shrivelled instantly.

'It seems a pity,' said Nathaniel, 'but as they seem to *want* to do it so much, I can't feel very unhappy about them, can you?'

'No,' said the boy. 'They want to get into the flame just as much as you want to get to the river.'

'But I,' said Nat, 'don't kill myself in getting there.'

'You might one day, if you wanted it too much,' replied the boy.

'Rubbish, I can swim!' said Nat, rather boastfully, for though in this river he could swim like a fish, in any other waters he could only struggle as far as his first breath would carry him. The river boy was silent: half his attention was elsewhere. He peered at everything they passed, in hopes of finding something out-of-the-way for the Miller.

They found a single, very early glow-worm in a hedge, and wasted a great deal of time and candle-power looking for others. 'If only we could get a handful—enough for him to fill his lantern with, so that he could read his old books by glow-worm light! *That* would be the very thing to please him.' But they found no more, and left the solitary one where it was.

'You never know, it may be there for a signal light. We are not the only ones who use this path.'

'Who else comes here?' asked Nat, inquisitive again. But as he spoke, a little owl stopped pretending to be a knob of wood, and flew down and brushed his cheek softly with his wing, and disappeared ahead of them down the path.

When Nat recovered from the start it gave him, the river boy was kneeling by a wild daffodil with a very heavily bowed head. He tapped it, and a faint, bothered buzzing came from inside.

'I thought so,' he said, and shook it again. Out came a protesting honey-bee, backwards, dizzy with sleep, and flew off slowly over the fields, hanging its legs.

'After him!' cried the boy, and darted away. 'He'll go to his nest, and a lump of wild honey-comb will be the very thing for the Miller!'

Nat scurried after, his lamp went out, and he got tangled up in briars, and hot and out of breath. And so the boy had to wait for him, and they lost the bee and wandered about in a pine copse, and found nothing. At last they came upon a stump where sat a fat old badger, licking his forepaw, with smears of honey and wax all over his head. This was the first badger Nat had ever seen, although their big mounds and doorways surrounded Bourne in the thickets. It looked unexpectedly large and fierce and foreign in its vivid black and white stripes. But the river boy was not at all in awe of it. Indeed, as soon as he saw the great creature he flew into a rage and stamped his foot. 'No hope of honey now!' he stormed. 'Greedy old, stripy old, fuzz-tailed *pig*! Where's our honey *for the Miller*?' At first the badger had been quite undisturbed as he sat there, rocking himself backwards and forwards, sucking his paw. But at mention of the Miller he looked crestfallen. At any rate, he took his paw out of his mouth in a hurry and lumbered off to a big hollow tree nearby, where he poked his head into a hole. A thin, distracted hum greeted him, but there was nothing left except a few sulky bees, and a trickle of dark honey down the bark. The badger was stung on his nose for his pains, and nursed it with his tongue, curling it first round one side, then (when it got tired) round the other. While he was attending to this he was stung on the eye too, which closed up and began to trickle tears.

'Think of something else!' said the boy imperiously. Nathaniel was more sympathetic and ventured to stroke the great beast behind his ear. 'Poor thing, what a bother.' But the badger suddenly set off with an idea, shunting away backwards without bothering to turn about; for badgers can go backwards as fast as forwards. Nat toppled over and was carried away, clutching at the heedless animal's fur. He was half-dragged, half-trundled out of the wood into a meadow, where the badger trotted to and fro sniffing loudly, rather like the pig he had so rudely been called.

Presently there was a grunt, and two shouts of joy. The

badger had found what he was seeking, and certainly it was the most unlikely thing to find growing among primroses in an April field. The last light of the river boy's lamp shone on the smooth pale buttons of a ring of young mushrooms. Most of them were tight and round—only a few hours old. The river boy forgave the badger and made him a garland of primroses in which he looked charming and a little silly. Then the boy picked a bunch of rushes, laid some in a star on the grass, and began to weave the others round and round them, twisting them in and out like wicker-work. He turned in the edges, plaited a handle, and in no time had a green-smelling basket to lay the buttons in. The boys took a short cut back to the river, and waved good-bye to the badger, who wrinkled up his swollen nose and nodded at them patiently, then backed away. With one pace into the shadows, he had vanished. His striped coat made him invisible, for by now there was enough starlight to throw striped shadows faintly between the silver stems of the young oaks. He was perhaps a little relieved to be rid of the boys, though pleased with his primrose collar.

As they reached the river-bank again they heard the sound of a weir. They moved towards it, and before long there was a light ahead—a light round and yellow as the eye of an owl.

SEVEN

The Miller's Supper

THE river widened suddenly into a broad pool, fringed about with ranks of flags, and by the weir, where the water fell roaring, stood a tumble-down stone building. It was partly thatched, partly tiled, and under it turned a dripping, groaning, weedy water-wheel. The mill stood, it seemed, almost *in* the river; for water flowed right underneath it through an arch. A bird flew, whistling, under this, and another, hooting, flew off a chimney-pot. It appeared that the owl and the kingfisher had both gone ahead to give news of their arrival. The round yellow light came from a bull's-eye window, high in the wall; and presently a door opened next to it, shining more light down a flight of rickety steps. Outlined in the doorway stood an enormously fat, short figure, with a cat on his shoulder, another in his arms, and a third twining about between his feet. One of the cats had no tail, one was spotted like a plum-pudding dog, and the third had fur so long its face was quite invisible. They were certainly odd enough—and this was certainly the Miller, for flour sifted down from every portion of his person. He was held together in various places by pieces of string—round his waist, criss-crossed round his trouser-legs, and lacing up his big apron at the back. For the rest, he just *bulged*. His head was fortunately bald, but his thick bushy eyebrows and every crease of his clothes gave off flour as a puffball spurts brown dust when you stamp on it. 'Nathaniel!' he exclaimed. 'What a pleasure, m'dear!' as if he had known him all his life.

'As for *you*'—turning to the river boy, who was looking unusually respectful—'what've become of the seven white sacks in the inner chamber? And where've 'ee been, and no work done since Saturday last?' His eyebrows drew together in a frown, and as he wagged his fat finger at the boy, flour shot off them like snow off the eaves, leaving them surprisingly black in his huge, round, moony face.

Nat pricked up his ears. Did the river boy work for the Miller then? Did he really live here? Was this where he spent his time whenever they were not together? But then where did he go on days when even the Miller did not know what he was doing? Apparently the boy sometimes gave him, too, the slip.

The boy did not like to be scolded, any more than the badger had done, and ran up the steps without a word, to hold out his basket in the light.

When the Miller saw what it held, he threw up his hands in delight. His whole frame shook, the three cats purred like kettles on the boil, the Miller rumbled and purred himself.

'Mushrooms! Quite, quite totally the wrong time of year! Oh, m'dears, what a present! Come in by, come in.' He took up the basket tenderly, and beckoned them in.

The upper room they entered was much the same as the round white room Nathaniel had imagined the inside of his head to be. It was warmly lit by a dancing fire, and by three quivering candles on the table. One circular window looked upstream. This was the one whose light had been their guide. Another, just like it, overlooked the wild water below the fall. The floor shook to the laborious turning of the wheel and the grinding of the millstones, which must be directly underneath them. From either window, by craning his neck round, Nat could see the wheel lazily turning in the darkness, lifting one by one its wet slats dripping with green slime, and shaking drops off on to the families of ferns that hung down out of every crack in the wall.

'Supper *first*,' said the Miller, 'then what you please—you shall see it all.'

The river boy moved about the room as though he knew it well, and whistled as if he loved this place. Nathaniel made himself small on the window-seat, because the Miller seemed to fill quite half the room: his shadow spread over all the ceiling. Besides, the room was unnecessarily full of furniture. Nat sat down on a sea-worn black chest with a skull and crossbones burnt on it with a poker. The boy then put a three-legged stool for himself, and a rocking-chair for the Miller. From a cupboard by the fireplace he took the oddest assortment of crockery and knives and spoons. The candlesticks were tall shells, and the cups were polished coconuts set in silver. The spoons were two of them carved from crystal—with a bent tin kitchen tea-spoon, to make up the number. The knives had handles of wonderful carved ivory, but their blades were old and chipped, and stained as black as Mrs. Dill's vegetable-scraper. The boy peeled the mushrooms, and then stood on the stool and reached down an oval mirror with an elaborate gilt frame. He poured some oil upon it, put the mushrooms in, and then started to fry them over the flames.

When Nat had done gaping at this remarkable sight, he turned, and saw that while the Miller sat waiting for his supper, he was squinting at Nathaniel through first one and then another of a collection of small empty picture-frames that hung upon a nail. All over the window-sill were scattered half-shells of birds'-eggs—speckled thrush-eggs, pure blue hedge-sparrow's eggs—even the minute freckled eggs of robin and wren. Each one held a drop of colour, every shade imaginable. The Miller then began to paint a picture—or at least appeared to be doing so. He had no palette, he never mixed his paints, he painted with a drop from one shell, a touch from another, glancing all the while at Nathaniel, the brush engulfed in one of his bunches of huge fingers and the little empty frame swallowed up in the other. The extraordinary thing was that he must have been painting upon the air itself, for there was no paper or canvas in the frame at all.

Nathaniel stroked the brushes, standing stuck in a cow's horn. They too were all of different shades.

'That one,' said the Miller, singling out a very small yellow-tipped one, 'is made of the very first hairs that fell off your head. Everything comes to the Mill.'

At this moment the river boy put the sizzling mirrorful of mushrooms under the Miller's nose, to see if it was done to his liking. Then began a great bustle, with the Miller booming out orders, and passing dishes in from his little stone-roofed larder. This was plastered on to the outside of the mill like a swallow's nest, close to the splashing wheel. The only way into the larder was through a window in the wall of the passage, and the Miller now stood with head and shoulders stuffed through this window, passing back dish after dish to the boys.

Presently he backed out and told Nathaniel to draw up his seat to the table.

'Only a very poor small meal, m'dear,' he sighed over the groaning table, 'but I couldn't be sure when you would be arriving. Some come early, some at a snail's pace—all I can promise *you* is a snail's appetite.'

And at that, Nat became aware that he was really very hungry indeed. Never had he seen or dreamt of a feast so queer and delicious as the one they now sat down to, with the firelight leaping round the room, and the three cats purring, and the millstones hissing, and the wheel creaking by, down below. They drank the clear dark soup out of curled shells. When Nathaniel's was empty, he put his to his ear, and could hear in it the sea roaring far, far away. As he listened to that faint surf he thought of his journey, of how one day he would stand on the shore and see the waves beat at his very feet. But as he looked about him he had little wish to be on his way to the sea. This was adventure enough—this warm moment in the bright-lit upper room, with the dark river murmuring and clucking all round the walls below, and the downstream window showing still one faint green bar of light in the west.

The Miller shot a sharp look at him, out of little blue eyes which hardly found room for themselves between the shaggy brows and the fat cheeks.

'One day, m'dear,' he said, though Nathaniel had not spoken of his journey. 'Time enough, time enough!'

The mirrorful of fried delicacies was put down on the table, but in the last few moments by the fire the Miller had made it up in the strangest manner. The sausages all stood on end, transformed into a row of Chinese mandarins with curling crisp gowns of bacon and broad mushroom hats upon their heads; one rode in a carriage with mushroom wheels and a mushroom parasol over his head. They were so marvellously made it seemed a pity to eat them, but once the three had begun, the whole procession vanished in a very short while.

As they were eating, the little owl came floating in through one window, soft as a moth. He perched on the corner of the table by the Miller's left hand, with his back to Nat, but turned his head round to stare at him comically. He swivelled it round so far it almost seemed that it must be fixed on a screw. Then this dumpy and exceedingly solemn little bird began to dance for his supper, lifting first one foot and then the other and slowly rocking from side to side. The Miller offered him a sausage almost as tall as himself.

'It's impossible!' thought Nat. But it was not. The bird swallowed most of it at a gulp—only a scrap of one end stayed sticking out of a corner of his open beak. After that he half-closed his eyes, and became as still as the pewter pepper-pot—except that now and then he would give a heave, when rather more of the sausage would disappear.

The green salad was made into a summer garden, with arbors of lettuce and a fountain playing oil and vinegar in the middle—Nat could not imagine how it was done. As for the fish dish, it was the oddest food that he had ever encountered: a crystal bowl like a rock-pool, fringed with weeds that could be eaten, and full of shrimps and shellfish of strong, curious flavours. In through the upstream window, like a bullet, came the kingfisher, just in time for this course, and he perched on the rim of the bowl to take his choice. Nat had never seen him so close before, glowing like a great jewel, slanting his big beak on one side with a look both fierce and funny. For though he was exquisitely beautiful, he was also short and stoutish and seemed as schoolboyish as the boys themselves.

Next, a roast peacock was brought in, dressed in its feathered coat, and in its beak a huge raisin soaked in brandy, burning blue. The tail was spread wide above the silver dish, and with it came a fleet of sauceboats and outlandish vegetables.

Much later, all three leant back from the table with sighs of satisfaction. By then the tower of fruit was scattered on the table, and nutshells lay everywhere. The last sips of clear pale wine were taken dreamily. The kingfisher had tucked his head so far under his wing, it was hard to tell which end of him was which. And the yellow eyes of the little owl were only just ajar. He had stopped heaving. The sausage was evidently growing comfortable.

The river boy loaded a tray with the tottering pile of crockery, and Nathaniel wondered who would wash it all up. But the boy simple threw the whole pile out of the downstream window to the fishes.

'Clutter, clutter, clutter, m'dear,' exclaimed the Miller drowsily, as the last spoon tinkled down among the stones far below. 'Every now and then I have to throw a whole cupboardful of junk out of that window or I should have no room to work in at all. The trouble is, of course, that afterwards I find I have thrown away my treasures, and kept *this* sort of thing!' He held up a thumbed, greasy, dog-eared, sixpenny account book, full of indecipherable sums and figures.

'That was in a whole chestful of pearls—I used to bark my shins on it in the passage—such a lot of pearls, rose and silver and black, some as big as peas they were, bags and bags full, as well as the dear knows how many necklaces, bracelets, tiaras, earrings, pendants and collars. But then it was all so much in the way. So out I tipped it—and meaning to keep back the prettiest, but this was all I found I had left!'

He leant so far back in the rocking-chair, it looked as though he were going to tip himself out as well. Only the window was so small, he would certainly have stuck in it. He rubbed his turnip of a nose mournfully, staring up into the shadows cast by the firelight on the ceiling.

'Not that it's *all* loss, by any means,' he brightened. 'Do you see my boat?' Leaning out as far as he could, Nathaniel could make out, among the flag-beds of the weir-pool, a crazy old flat-bottomed boat, half-full of rainwater and last year's leaves. 'Sometimes,' said the Miller, 'I go fishing, and one day I caught *this*, m'dear—worth many a chestful of pearls to me.' He unhooked from the shadowy wall a delicate harp, only a handspan high and made of some greenish gold carving, in the shape of a girl with a fish's tail, and her hair fanned out as she combed it, to make its golden wires. The Miller stroked them with his clumsy-looking fingers, which all the same never touched anything without grace and skill. He put his head on one side, and began to sing to the faint, thready twangling of the harp, in a voice astonishingly small and warbling. Nat thought it must come from very far inside his bulk: like the voice of the little boy he must once have been—now shut up inside the huge man. Both harp and voice together were only just loud enough to drown the monotonous roar of the weir. He sang one song after another. Some were nursery rhymes and ballads Nat's mother had sung to him, some were sea-shanties and soldiers' favourites, such as Grandfather would whistle in his bath on a fine morning. But many of them he did not know. Some haunted him with their melody, or their strange, wild words—some were so ludicrously bad that he could hardly keep a straight face. But the Miller did not seem to pick and choose at all; they all came out of him like beads on a thread—or like the thread itself, reeling out of a spider. The gold wires of the Naiad harp trembled, the flame of the fire died low. Through the singing Nat could hear the millstones mumbling under his feet, and the small snoring of the little owl. The last song was a lullaby—or at least the last

Nat heard; for his head, which had been nodding for a long while, found a comfortable place on the window-sill among various treasures of the Miller's, and he fell fast asleep.

EIGHT
The Water-Mill

NATHANIEL woke up next morning a moment before he opened his eyes. The first thing he was aware of was a delicious dry smell—something between bread and fresh straw. There was another smell too—a wet one—something like damp stones and ferns. He lay and sniffed. Mrs. Dill must be using some very odd rubbish to light the fire with in the kitchen. Whatever it was, it smelt very like the Miller's cornmeal, and the river. And with that, the whole of the evening before rushed into his memory with a pang of sharp disappointment. Surely, surely he could have kept awake a little longer, listening to the Miller's songs! There was so much he had planned to do there with the river boy while he had sat dreaming on the old sea-chest in the upper room. That weir-pool—and the boat waiting, asking for a voyage. And he had never seen the millstones, nor any of the rest of the dishevelled old building. And what gave him such a pang was this. He knew by now that once he had left the river he never returned to it at the same place. On the next visit he would find himself farther downstream. Nor would it do to turn back in the middle of a journey to the sea. Perhaps, even if he tried to go back, he would never find those earlier stopping-places again. He could not tell why, but he felt this strongly. He would, in fact, have been afraid to try.

All this passed through his mind in the moments after waking. He lay with eyes clenched shut, and with such vivid pictures of the Mill and the Miller in his mind that he was able to pretend he was really there. He did not want to open his eyes on the familiar low white ceiling with its tiresomely familiar pattern of cracks. He knew by heart the shapes they made—a long-nosed witch—a boot—and a spouting whale. He was tired of all the stories he had invented about them.

There must be a high wind in the yew-trees, he thought, for they were once more trying to deceive him with the sound of a weir. It must also be uncommonly sunny; for a great brightness glowed through his eyelids. A fine Spring morning at Bourne, with a high wind, was not a thing to be despised, however inferior to the river's secret valleys, and so at last Nat did open his eyes and take his ears out of the deep, smothery nest he always made for them, by pulling the corners of his pillow high up over the edge of the blankets.

He opened his eyes and sat bolt upright in one movement—to get it over. And then his eyes blinked shut again in surprise, and his mouth fell open instead! The only ceiling was a brilliant blue air that stung his sleepy eyelids. Not a breath of wind stirred. The noise of a weir was in joyful fact—the noise of a weir: a babble and roar of laughing, rushing, spinning water. The smell of meal and wet stones was as real as his own nose, and he himself was curled up in a huge old seven-bushel corn-measure of ancient green bell-metal, half-full of straw, and with a fine, soft white sack stuffed with dried thyme for a pillow. The measure was placed on the wooden platform at the top of the Mill steps. The three cats, looking more freakish than ever in the early-morning sunshine, sat each on a different step, washing their ears.

Best of all, there stood the Miller himself in the open doorway. For it was he who had just carried out the corn-measure with the sleeping Nathaniel in it, and had set it down where the sun would wake him.

Nat was so overjoyed that he leapt up, and clasped in his wide-flung arms a small part of the curve of the Miller's middle, much as one might try to hug for joy the trunk of a hundred-year-old beech-tree! Flour flew about in clouds at their rapturous 'Good-mornings', for the Miller seemed as delighted as Nat; and when he laughed the whole platform quaked, and the stairs trembled right down to the lowest mossy step. The cats sprang up and began to mew: the kingfisher whistled by among the yellow flags, and an industrious noise of a broom from somewhere indoors ended with the clatter of a flung-away dust-pan, as the river boy wriggled out under the Miller's elbow to join them.

'Oh, I've never been so happy in all my life!' exclaimed Nat. 'Can I stay here? How long can I stay? I want to stay for ever and ever!'

'Don't ask how long, m'dear. Most unwise thing to think about!' said the Miller sharply, and 'Never, never ask' ran the water under the arch with a warning voice.

Even as the words came out of Nathaniel's mouth a strange transparency had begun to steal through the solid shapes of things around him, as if thinning them away from behind. The Mill, the weir-pool, the very Miller himself, all quivered as reflections do when some current rises from below but has not yet broken the surface into ripples.

Nat resolutely filled his mind with the sound of the river, and shut away anxious thoughts. He stopped trying to make certain of anything more than *now*—this moment that he was in the midst of. However long, however brief, this *now* was his. That was what he told himself urgently. And as he looked down the valley of the river he loved, the transparency withdrew: everything became as solidly real again as ever.

The river boy took his hand and swung him down the steps on to the bank. Thick white dew in large drops lay on the grass, as if the Miller had thrown out another chestful of pearls. They went round the back of the Mill, where the trees on the edge of a wood leant over the sagging tiled roof. Chestnuts were spreading out green fans, and wood-anemones covered the ground—starry where the sun had reached them, half-closed like broken birds' shells in the shadow of the Mill's dank North wall. The downstream wall looked out on a spit of shore slanting away below the weir, and covered with kingcups. In one bare place between their clumps lay an old ring of charred pebbles. The river boy knelt down and built this old fireplace into shape again. He tested the direction of the breeze by holding up his wet forefinger, and wedged a strong stake into the overhanging bank.

Such preparations delighted Nat, who had never had a *breakfast* picnic in his life. He filled the kettle and stood it by the stake. Then he ran about collecting bleached dry driftwood, and the Miller threw him a loaf out of the window, still warm from the oven, and golden and crusty. It was a very small one though, hardly bigger than a bun, and Nat privately hoped there would be at least one each, the fresh morning made him so hungry.

Hanging from a hazel branch was a row of silver and freckled trout—fresh-caught—someone must have hooked them in the mists of daybreak. They seemed now to dance in the shimmer of heat that went up from the brisk bonfire. The kettle on the stake was quite wrapped up in the roaring flames and all at once was bursting with steam, hissing like a little dragon. The boy made porridge and cups of steaming chocolate, and then fried the fish—all before Nat had finished washing his face in the river and saying his prayers; which had gone unsaid, he remembered, the night before. The two sat side by side on the green bank among the primroses, staring over the brims of their hot mugs at the flashing, churned-up river below the fall. The Miller did not come to breakfast; they could hear his ponderous footsteps busy somewhere indoors. Nat wondered in what part of that queer, tall, hunched-up building he himself had spent the night. Not a dream came back to him from all those hours of sleep. And where did the river boy sleep? And what huge bed heaved and sank at nights under the Miller's snores? What happened to the Mill while everyone slept? Did the millstones turn on with nothing to grind?

While they munched, Nat counted the kingfisher nine times as it flew down past the Mill, dipping over the fall—and nine times up again. The upstream journeys were a little slower and more careful, for then his beak was full—generally with a minnow. 'How very fast he must fish!' exclaimed Nat. 'He's only gone a minute each time.'

'That's not always *him*, sometimes it's *her*. Look! That's her—and that's him!' This time two brilliant blue balls came spinning round the bend together. They looked exactly alike to Nat, but the river boy knew them apart. 'It's quite easy,' he said, 'once you know—*his* feathers never lie so neatly as hers, she spends so much more time preening herself.' But Nathaniel could not distinguish any feathers at all at that distance—the birds seemed each made of a single blue coal that flickered into green and then dulled into red.

'Have they a nest? Can we see it? Would they desert it if we went close?'

'None of the birds here will be afraid of you. Every one of them feeds on the scraps from the Mill.'

At that moment Nathaniel had just realized the cause of a great pother on the roof. The Miller's full-moon face appeared among the chimney-pots, thrust out through a skylight. He was spreading crumbs and corn before a whistling, whirling, chattering cloud of thrushes and pigeons and robins.

It reminded Nat that he had already eaten three generous slices of the Miller's little loaf, and so had the river boy. Yet the loaf—so small it sat upon a young sycamore leaf—still seemed but half cut. It was very mysterious, and as he ate he stole secret glances now and then, to see if he could catch it in the act of swelling or puffing itself up like a frog. But if it did grow at all, it must have been as the hour hand steals round the clock, so slowly that it seems perfectly still each time you look at it. The river boy laughed at him, guessing his thoughts: 'What does the *size* have to do with it?—size makes no difference at all.' And he reached down a fisherman's bag from a branch, and put away the rest of the loaf. 'It will come in handy for lunch,' he said, and left Nat to wonder. Perhaps it would still be there at supper-time? He would not object: it was delicious.

They doused the fire with water from the river, and rinsed the mugs. And a yellow wagtail came running right to Nat's foot, closer than he had ever seen one before, and fluttered upon the rims of the mugs, drying them with dabs of his long tail. Mrs. Dill called the little birds 'Dishwashers' but he had never seen them at such work before. When this was done, two pigeons fell out of the top of a larch, with much fuss and clatter of wings, and took the handles of the mugs in their feet, and carried them straight to the upper room, through the window, and hung them on their hooks. A wild rabbit lolloped down and sat on his haunches, the sun shining pink through his ears. His front teeth flashed up and down like the needle of a sewing-machine, while the broad leaves which the boys had used as plates went headlong down his throat—butter and crumbs as well, for a relish. So breakfast was cleared away, in less time than it takes to tell.

The boy then said he must work till noon, so Nat went along to help him. By a great downstair door, big enough to drive a cart through, they went into the gloom of the chamber where the millstones were grinding. Somewhere outside, the Miller was altering the flow of water through the weir hatches, and the huge round stones, hissing against each other, began to turn faster. The river boy climbed to the loft and began to empty sacks of corn into the ancient wooden hopper, while Nathaniel, standing down below, beside the corn-measure in which he had awoken that morning, hooked fresh sacks on to a rope for him to haul up. The three cats whisked and pounced in the mealy gloom, the floor trembled, the roar of the water and noise of the wheel sent Nathaniel into a dream. He changed places after a while with the river boy and could not take his eyes off the swirl of grain sinking through the hopper like the sand through Mrs. Dill's egg-timer. On the wall above his head hung a real old hour-glass, a huge affair, and above it a great sickle. Both of them looked very ancient; but the sickle's blade was sharp enough, as he found when he ran his thumb along it. Someone, too, must have tipped up the hour-glass only a moment before; for almost all the sand was in the upper half, sifting slowly through.

The grain they ground was of many different kinds. Nat knew wheat and oats and barley and rye and maize, but there were all kinds of other seeds he had never seen—large three-cornered grains, others as tiny as poppy-seed, some flat and round, some bean-shaped, some with hooks. And besides the big sacks which the boy brought him, all round the walls stood others that smelt foreignly of spices.

'Everything comes to the Mill,' the Miller had said last night —but who brought it? Had the Miller some other man to help him besides the river boy? It would need someone stronger, and with a longer sweep of arm, to wield *that* sickle.

'Shall I ever see the fields where this grows?' asked Nat, afraid to ask a more direct question, knowing he would get no answer if he did. He plunged his fingers into the coolness of a heap of wheat, more gold than any he had seen around Bourne.

'Yes,' replied the boy, 'the fields are on our way. We shall find them on either side of it.'

'Then,' thought Nathaniel, 'I shall keep my eyes open for the reaper.' But he did not say so.

The morning wore on towards noon, and stronger and stronger fingers of sunlight poked through cracks and knot-holes and pointed across the dusty air. Nathaniel's arms ached a little with lifting and pouring the heavy sacks; for now the Miller had come to help them, and the sacks came swinging up and plumped beside him quicker than he could empty them. Suddenly he saw something black fall into the hopper, and he plunged in his arm after it, afraid that it might be a bat—there were clusters of them, hanging by their toes along the rafters.

'Mind now, m'dear,' said the Miller, taking a good grasp of

his shorts. 'It's early days to go into the hopper yourself!' and dragged him back. Nat saw that what had fallen in was the tiny dark frame in which the Miller had so carefully painted a picture of airy nothing while they waited for supper. It was now just disappearing through the bottom of the hopper, and he ran down the ladder to the stones below in order to take out the splinters that would be falling into the flour. There was no hope, he thought, of anything but smithereens coming out from between the great smooth stones.

He waited for a long while, watching the trickling meal slip from their lips, but—no splinters appeared! Surely the frame must have come through by now? Then he caught sight of it— lying in the flour like a present in a bran-tub. He snatched it out and blew on it. Not a corner was even chipped! And there, where mere emptiness had been, was a delicate miniature, painted on glass. He took it to the door and stood owlishly staring at it. The painting was a tiny likeness of himself, sitting at the round window in the upper room of the Mill. It was full of waving shadows and firelight, and through the round window appeared a dark landscape no bigger than a coin; and in it the silver thread of the river could just be seen. But how had the Miller painted, in that one minute window, such miles and miles of dark mountains—such thick thousands of pinprick stars? And how had he made the river seem to wind right away through eternity?

'Did you *know* it was there? Could you see it before?—when you were painting it, I mean?' Nat asked.

The Miller was looking over his shoulder, rubbing his forehead. 'Not plainly, m'dear; in a way I saw it, in a way this is the first minute I've clapped eyes on it. Does it please you, then?'

'It's *beautiful*,' said Nat seriously. 'I think you must be a very famous artist.'

At that the Miller chuckled hugely. 'M'dear, I *am*!'

'Is it mine—to keep, I mean?' asked Nat.

'Yes, 'tis yours—but mine to keep. I'll keep it for you.' So saying he took it upstairs and drove in a new silver nail and hung it on the crowded walls of the upper room, among his thousand other treasures.

In his own mind, Nat was a little uneasy lest in one of the Miller's periodic spring-cleanings he should absent-mindedly throw it out of the window. But he felt it would not be polite to hint at such a thing, and the picture certainly seemed to belong in this room. So there it remained, hanging dark and secret, with the upper edge of its frame still white with flour.

NINE

The Mill-Pool

ONE of the other pictures in the Miller's room was of a town beside a river—though whether this river or another one, Nat could not say. It was a town crowded with steeples and towers. On one belfry the dial of a clock showed oddly bright and clear in the light of a full moon, painted among romantic clouds in the corner. Just as it dawned on Nathaniel that the hands of the clock were not painted at all, but made of real brass, there came a dusty whirring from behind the frame, and then a thin, breathlessly fast striker ting-tinged out the twelve strokes of noon. The picture was in fact the front of a clock, all the wheels and works tucked away behind the frame. But whatever hour of night or day the real clock in the painted tower might tell in this manner, the time in the town remained moonrise.

In the room below Nat's feet the millstones were slowing down, and less water was rushing through the sluices. The boy was calling him out into the sunshine; and work was over for the day. At least it was over for *them*; though what the Miller might do from noon till nightfall was nobody's business but his own.

Nathaniel remembered again the unsolved problem of the Miller's rooms. When outside the Mill, he had only counted, so far, the two windows of the upper room, the big downstair door of the granary and grindstone chamber, and the little door up the steps at the side. These, together with the skylight through which the Miller fed the birds, and the window into the outdoor larder, seemed to be the only openings anywhere in all these many-angled walls, unless one counted the archway right under the Mill. But surely such a multitude of odd levels of roof must hide more rooms than he had seen. Were they without windows or doors? What puzzled him still more was that at certain moments, when someone was talking, or when his attention was distracted by a passing bird—moments when he was not actually looking at the Mill, but had it in the corner of his eye—he had seemed to catch the gleam of sunlight on other windows. And once, he was almost sure, a small dark door had opened silently, just by the wheel, its sill upon the water's edge and its reflection below. But when he counted again there were still only the doors and windows that he knew, and nothing at all to account for the shadowy stir of opening and shutting, coming and going, that he had sensed a moment before. Perhaps it was all a trick of the ceaselessly turning wheel which made the whole building tremble on its foundations over the gliding flow.

The river boy had dragged the old boat out of the shallows, and had it upside down on the bank, caulking its starting seams with odd ends of tarry rope. The bottom was all bearded with green slime and smelt unpleasant. But to Nat it was perfection; for he had never been in a boat at all; Bourne was too far inland. When he was a tiny boy he had spent many hours punting himself up and down the corridor's long blue carpet, in the big bottom drawer of his mother's tallboy, with a broom-handle for a pole. A real boat, however leaky and stinking, filled this glorious morning to the brim of delight. He helped stuff the last cracks and scrape away the weed. There was even a cluster of fresh-water mussels attached under the stern, and he carried them off in a bunch, so as not to split up the family, thoughtfully finding them a good deep crack between two rocks.

'I do hope they will take root again nicely,' he said anxiously, 'or screw themselves in, or glue themselves up, whichever it is they do? It can't be a very *interesting* life, being a mussel. Just opening, I suppose, and shutting, every now and then.'

This reminded him again of the mysterious windows and door and as he sat scraping away at the end of the boat he said in a casual voice, 'I suppose it must be very cosy at night for you and the Miller to lie in bed and listen to the weir as you go to sleep? —when your bedroom windows are open, I mean. I suppose you would hear the water very plainly, almost *anywhere* in the Mill?'

But the river boy looked at him under his eyelashes, amusedly, and Nat realized that the train of his thoughts had been quite obvious.

'Who says I *go* to sleep at night? Or the Miller either? What is to prevent him working all night? The river doesn't go to sleep, nor the wheel. Why should we?'

'Well, *does* the Miller go to bed? He must go to sleep *some time*—so must you!'

'I don't see why, necessarily,' said the boy provokingly. 'Why should one? I might fly about all night like a will-o'-the-wisp— and as for a bed, there are so many sorts of beds—river-beds for instance!'

Nat jumped at him in exasperation, and they tussled on the boat and nearly fell into the river.

'Come on, let's turn her over and push her off; I have so much to show you—secret places!' That was enough to side-track Nat—one secret was as good as another. If the boy would not answer his questions, there would be something else equally exciting.

So they pushed off, stowing under the thwarts some apples

and the bag with the loaf in it and a hunk of cheese. They steered for the middle of the great weir-pool, keeping well away from the dangerous suck of the fall itself. Nathaniel sat in the bows, paddling inexpertly and excitedly like a duckling, with an old sky-blue paddle, while the river boy stood on the stern-boards and punted with long, easy thrusts of a very tall slender pole. Yet tall as it was, out in the centre he could no longer touch bottom with it, and they drifted dreamily on, as though in the midst of blue air; for the pool was so still it seemed itself to be only the lower part of a bottomless sky. Blue dragonflies with black wings darted round them, and friendly water-boatmen sculled alongside, dimpling the water's skin with their feet, but never breaking the surface.

'How marvellous they are!' murmured Nat, leaning over the side to watch. 'Just walking on the water. Don't you *wish* you could do that?'

The river boy looked at him oddly, without replying, but took up his pole again and punted on, leaving the little boatmen far behind. When they drew near the opposite shore, Nat realized it was not the real bank at all, but a strip of mud, fringed with reeds and crowned by a crest of pussy-willows in full yellow pollen. Beyond this lay a second arm of the pool, and in the middle of that was an island. It rose up steeply in white rocks, and the top of it was covered with wild fruit-trees in blossom. There were gnarled, stubby apple-trees in coral-coloured bud, and a pear-tree like a white cloud after a shower. And overtopping the rest there were tall cherry-trees with droop-ing flowers, that showed hardly any more colour than raindrops, among the still half-leafless branches.

In the southern cliff, which was soft and sandy, and not much higher than Nat's head, were dozens of round holes. They were the homes of the sand-martins who flickered all about them. As the old boat drifted close under the shore, the sand-martins' wives looked at them out of their doorways, with wide, mild faces.

They circled the whole island, and under the western cliff they found rushes, and an untidy moorhen's nest with five sooty chicks bobbing about like corks in the ripple from the punt's bows. They came right into Nat's hand and pattered over the palm and plopped off his fingers, with their queerly big feet sprawling—all peeping with wild excitement and welcome. The mother just clucked encouragingly and seemed to think they were in no danger.

The northern cliff held a dipper's nest, set in a cranny, with a porch of fine moss built out over it. Nat was able, by standing up in the punt, to put a crumb into each of the five mouths of the nestlings, that gaped, together, like five trap-doors on a single spring, as the shadow of his hand fell across them. The fat father dipper stood on a stone in the water and ducked and bowed and seemed much obliged.

Last of all, on the eastern side, the river boy pointed out to Nathaniel a hole with a lime-whitened perching-place beside it, where one or two fish-scales shone. Out of it like two bullets shot the screaming kingfishers. So *that*, then, was where at least one of his supper-companions had slept last night!

'The little owl's nest,' the boy murmured, continuing Nat's thought, 'is in that apple-tree up there, but they won't want to be disturbed on such a bright day.'

Nat sighed for perfect content; never in all his hunts had he found so many nests at once, and never before had he looked in upon nestlings or sitting birds without some shadow of guilt; for though he seldom took eggs, he was always afraid the mothers might desert their nests because he had been near. He hated to see them brave out his soft approach as long as they dared, and then at the last moment flit away in deadly fear.

Now the boy made the boat fast to a branch, and they clambered up the steep little cliffs, pulling themselves up by apple branches. The top was perfectly flat and covered with very fine grass, soft as hair. They sprawled under the pear-tree to eat their bread and apples, and whether the loaf was ever finished or not Nat never learned, for they kept throwing up handfuls of crumbs into the air to see the sand-martins catch them like jugglers before any fell to the ground. 'I thought they only liked flies,' said Nat. 'It must be fly-bread. Do you make flour for squashed-fly biscuits at the Mill?'

The river boy made a face at him. Then they wanted to feed all the other birds again, and finally they lay leaning over the edge where the cliff sloped down, dropping scraps to the fish.

'Teach me how to tickle trout,' begged Nat, sure the river boy would know. The boy showed him. Very patiently, very slowly, he slid his arm deep into the water near a shadowy trout and moved it by inches nearer. His fingers curved below its body so gradually that the water never stirred. When he actually touched the nervy, silvery side, surely the fish would dart away? But no, the boy began to rub it very softly, just behind the gills, and the fish even arched against the finger a little, like a cat, in his enjoyment. Lower and lower the fingers worked, till in a flash they closed the last fraction of an inch and drew out the astonished and affronted trout, flipping and thrashing on the grass! They dropped him in again and he flicked away under water. Perhaps he was warned for the future to beware of unexplained delicious sensations, or perhaps he thought it all a bad daydream, or perhaps he felt, like Nathaniel, transported for a moment to a world he had often wanted to enter, and set back in his own world against his will.

Nat tried to do the same, all round the island, and caught only one trout in all the long afternoon. At last, with his arm still trailing in the water, he fell asleep, a half-sleep in which he was still aware of birds singing and all the slight sounds of growing leaves on the island, over his head. Presently he was aware, too, of shadows growing cooler and also that he was alone. He sat up, a little bewildered, for it was growing dusk and the island orchard looked very different now: he could hardly tell blossom from leaf, and the birds were still. A mist began to rise under the trees. It was so quiet, he did not like to go about hallooing for the river boy, but found himself walking almost on tiptoe round the island. There was nobody left on it but himself, yet how the boy could have stolen away Nat could not imagine, for the old boat was still moored to its branch, though the bows had swung gradually out from the shore in the push of the current.

So at last, wondering, and a little scared at the thought of guiding the punt alone, he swung himself down into it, untied the rope, and pushed off towards the junction of the two pools. He thought he could see a glimmer beyond the row of willows, and this would be the light from the Mill, no doubt. It had been such a long, long Spring day: he was curiously tired. The old punt nosed along softly like a grazing beast across the flat water. He did not find the pole too difficult to manage, though he drew it out rather jerkily each time, hand over hand, and sometimes nearly toppled over with its weight, and he dared not stand upon the very end of the boat as the boy had done, for fear of falling in altogether. Each time he plunged the pole in, the boat gave an encouraging swoop forward, ruffling up the water a little. Bats flickered all about him with their thin voices, so close to the very edge of hearing that he sometimes doubted whether he really heard them at all: they seemed to be only a pricking in his skull. They could almost have been the sound of starlight itself, a high, thin clicking as one by one the stars pricked through the green dusk. For it was an evening as slow and clear as yesterday's.

Star-gazing, and listening to the bats, Nathaniel had drifted to the very corner of the narrow islet of willows, and was just coming round into the weir-pool itself. He had forgotten to punt for some time. The boat was moving on with the current now, and he never asked himself what current it was, and where it would lead him.

Across the water stood the Mill, all in inky shadow from the wood. He must have been mistaken about the lights, for the windows, after all, were not yet lit. But surely, now, he could see that extra door open at the water's edge? He strained his eyes but could not be certain in the twilight.

Then a smaller shadow stole away from that dark blot which might be a door. It skimmed, upright, across the water, to and fro, darting and hovering. What could it be—too tall and thin for a bird flying, too quick for a sail? He sat breathlessly watching and with heart beating fast, not heeding the sound of the loudening water—feeling every moment more alone on its great dark sheet, where this strange quick thing would float and run as if it could never tire. It paused at last, upright in the middle of the pool. Nat heard a tiny sharp sound like a match being struck. The shadowy thing seemed smaller now, crouching down close to the surface. Presently it stood up again and turned. It was a figure, and whoever it was had been *kneeling on the water.* In its hand it held a small bowl of shaking light—a clay lamp! The flame cast up its glare upon the face, and it was the face of the river boy. But not as Nathaniel had ever seen it. The light sharply illuminated his pointed chin and cheeks and left the eyes dark. Intent, rapt beyond any knowledge of Nathaniel's presence near him, the boy stood gazing down into the light, his feet on the water. In that moment Nathaniel had a glimpse of all he had so longed to know—what the river boy was like and what he did when he was alone, quite by himself, not working for the Miller or making company for Nathaniel. But of what his thoughts might be, that intent, secret, candle-lit face gave away no sign.

Now he was moving once again, and he began to glide about at his soundless solitary play, running on the surface of the pool, his lamp in his hand. In spiralling circles he swung out farther and farther. Now, this very next time, he would pass right by the boat. Nathaniel hardly knew whether to cry out to him, if he passed without seeing him, or to stay dumb; the boy looked so unlike the laughing, friendly companion who had tickled the trout. As he scudded nearer, though, with dreaming face and arms lit up, and all the rest of him almost invisible, Nat could bear no longer the remote stillness of his expression. Surely he could not have forgotten him so completely?

With a clumsy, fumbling movement, hardly knowing what he intended to do, he stood up in the boat and stretched out his arms. In a moment more he might have stepped right out of the boat himself, on to, or into, the water.

But at that instant the river boy lifted his head, and saw him, and for an endless moment they stared at each other, like utter strangers at the world's end. A look that might have been fear, or anger, or entreaty passed over the boy's face.

Then it seemed the world's end indeed. For all the while, in that deceptive stillness, the current had been drawing the boat very quietly towards the lip of the weir. Suddenly the bows swung round and out—over black, empty air. The roar of the weir rose up like a solid wall, and Nat was falling, falling, over the edge into nothingness.

*   *   *   *   *

When he opened his eyes he was walking through the dusk. In his hand he had his clay lamp. He had just lit it for the first time, and was bringing it back from the ash-tree to show his mother.

TEN

The Midsummer Corn

IT was Midsummer Day, and too sultry to do anything at all at Bourne. Mr. Greenaway drowsed as he leaned on his spade, Mrs. Dill twirled her mop languidly out of an upper window, and Grandfather was asleep on the stone slabs outside the drawing-room, with the paper over his head. Nathaniel's mother was picking lavender, or so she said, but really she was just drifting up and down the cooler parts of the higher garden, enjoying her flowers and thinking of those to come. Nat could see all this from where he lay curled up in his private look-out place, a nest of branches high up in a beech at the bottom of the lower garden. He could account for the movements of the whole household from there. Even Rough and Sly were visible to him, a toy dog asleep under the fig-tree and a toy cat asleep in the grilling heat of the yard.

If he looked downwards he saw the beech boughs growing out all round the bole, like a descending spiral staircase to the remote floor of the lawn. Forty feet below him in the border an enormous red June rose swayed on its stem, so bright in the hot glare that it dazzled his eyes, and the colour seemed to overflow the edges of the petals. There had been thunder yesterday, and it had gone mumbling round the sky all night, circling the valleys several times, yet never breaking outright into a storm. Now the clouds were beginning to mass up again with more determination, and birds and grasshoppers fell silent one by one. Nathaniel rocked his nest of boughs to and fro, and shouted to the slow, threatening clouds to hurry up. The light faded into scowling shadow; a cuckoo sounded with a breaking note, suddenly very loud, across the hay meadows, and then fell quiet. The great towers and bastions of cloud sailed over all the sky, and the thunder began again to growl.

Everyone else in the garden went indoors. Mrs. Dill even got into a cupboard in the kitchen for greater safety, for she was very much afraid of thunder. She left the door open a crack, though, because she was also afraid of suffocating; and through this crack Mr. Greenaway would pass her cups of tea to calm her twittering nerves.

'I don't know where Master Nat is, I'm sure I don't know where Master Nat is,' she bewailed in muffled tones from behind a barricade of biscuit tins. Mr. Greenaway soothed her, for he could see the top of the beech-tree shaking boisterously and knew Nathaniel was not far out of reach.

'I don't like to think of him struck by lightning, and him only just out of bed with his cold,' she went on, and it was of no use to tell her the storm was still twenty miles away. At every flicker of lightning she shrank farther back among the jars of pickles, and covered her ears with her hands.

Nat, on the other hand, was thoroughly enjoying himself,

shouting when the thunder roared, daring it to come close, and every time hopefully counting the seconds between the blink and the crash, to see if it were really going to pass overhead. It did draw nearer, and soon fat drops began to darken the pale slates of the roof, and smack down upon the beech leaves. He would be sheltered, though, for a little longer, and he pulled the branches closer round his head.

Mrs. Dill was more distressed than ever, for all the elements were equally terrible to her. 'Hark at it, just hark at it! Did you ever hear such rain in all your life?' She was determined on some catastrophe or other this morning, and would perhaps have preferred Mr. Greenaway to be a little more disturbed, and not just to sit there filling his black pipe, so much at his ease under the open window. She was sure his pipe would attract the lightning. 'Like comes to like, Mr. Greenaway, I said like to like—and lightning is such a nasty, chancy creature!'

But he would not put away his pipe, and indeed leant right out of the window to shout to Nat, who was at length being forced from his perch by the rain, and clambering down.

'Run quick, Master Nat, then,' Mr. Greenaway shouted. 'Run between the drops, then'—which was a favourite encouragement of his.

At that moment several things happened at once. A fork of brilliant lightning flashed down near the garden itself, there was an instant tearing crash of thunder that made even Mr. Greenaway draw in his head, and Nat, in excitement, jerked the small branch he was holding on to, so that it came away in his hand, leaving a long white scar upon the bark. He sat back with a bump on a lower branch, and out of the white scar, as if it had been a door, came walking the river boy.

'Come on,' he cried. 'We *will* run between the drops!' and seizing Nathaniel's hand, he jumped down with him, and they sped across the lawn through rain that fell so violently it looked like solid silver rods, or standing corn. Nathaniel could not feel his feet touch the ground, they were speeding along so fast—as quick almost as thought would carry them. And as they ran, the light, and the colours about them, changed from grey to gold.

When the breath was quite gone out of their bodies, they paused. Then Nathaniel saw, to his delight, that the whispering rods of rain had given way to real corn, standing all about them, as high as his head. He was still tingling with the excitement of the thunderstorm, and after its loud darkness the light and silence of the cornfield were strange and delicious.

He was sure they were close to the river by the faint smell in the air, so he began parting the tall wheat all round him. Yes, there it was, twinkling, only a step or two away. It flowed very deep and calm here, between its cornfields. Together they pushed through to the bank, and lay down. The river boy was shredding a head of corn, spitting out the chaff and eating the grains. Harvest must be earlier here, or the season later, for at Bourne the farmers were only haymaking and the corn was green. Here the wheat was already pale and ripe and the grains were hard.

'They look like funny little Egyptian mummies,' said Nathaniel, rolling a few grains in the palm of his hand. Lying on his elbow he stared into the corn as if it had been a forest. Poppies opened crumpled buds high up among the tops. Far down below, wild heartsease grew in multitudes; and scarlet pimpernels were already closing, to say it was past noon. A column of ants went marching away out of sight, straight down between the rows. For some time Nat poked about and squinted along the aisles of corn, swinging his heels in the air and not bothering to talk to the river boy; they were sharing a kind of contentment that needed no words. This was very reassuring; for after that visit to the Mill in the Spring Nathaniel had wondered sometimes if things might have altered between them. Ever since that glimpse of the river boy walking on the water, he had felt almost as though he had spied on his secret life. Would the boy, when they met again, trust him not to ask questions? Nathaniel was resolved never to refer to that glimpse, any more than he would have fingered the eggs of the kingfisher. He let the strange meeting sink into his mind, deep and unreturning like a stone into a pool.

The moment, though, that the boy came walking out of the

beech-tree and took his hand, Nathaniel knew that all was well, and that the boy felt as safe with him as ever. So now they idled happily together, before moving on.

Nathaniel could see that this was the same large and very golden grain which they had been grinding at the Mill. Now they had reached the fields where it grew, he began to wonder again about the great sickle he had seen hanging on the granary wall. Would they meet the reaper? He stood tiptoe on a stump by the water, and could just look over the tops of the wheat. There was no visible end to it. Rippling away and away, it rose and fell over little hillocks, poured round and under any trees that came in its way, and ran right on into the heat-haze at the foot of the encircling mountains. Perhaps it even flowed on among the mountains, seeping between them and spreading out into the lands beyond—that is, if there *was* a country beyond, and if the mountains were not the edge of everything, as Nat more than half believed.

There was no knowing whether they were now a long way from the Mill, or still quite near it. For though its tall, hunching shape and the chestnut wood behind it were not to be seen, there were many such clumps sprinkled far and near along the river's course.

'Do you like harvesting?' asked the boy, watching him.

'Oh *yes*! Only they never allow me to do more than hold the horses' heads. And that's never necessary, anyway: the horses all stop and start themselves. Whichever you want, you have only to say "Heugh!" and they do it! Are we going to harvest here?'

'Well, there is plenty we *could* harvest,' said the boy, in his casual way. 'Only we must begin where it's cut, of course.'

He stood up and began to saunter along the bank till they came to the mouth of a winding path that led away between the ranks of corn towards the mountains. Nathaniel followed in silence, a silence that became a little bored as the flinty path went on and on, with nothing to look at but the corn close to their faces on either side. Nat grew hot and thirsty. Harvesting seemed a less pleasant prospect. And anyway, when were they even going to begin? Just as he was ready to protest, they reached a thorn-tree growing by the path, with a patch of shadow on the grass underneath it. There they halted, and Nathaniel sat down, panting.

'Get up,' said the boy. 'You may be sitting on a hoofmark.'

'Well, what if I am?' retorted Nat a little shortly. 'It won't hurt me.'

'But *you* will hurt the hoofmark.—Yes, you were on one, and you have squashed it so I can't see which way it points.' He clambered up the tree briskly and looked round.

'What are you looking for?'

'A horse,' said the boy. 'We can't harvest without a horse.' At that Nat's interest revived, for he loved horses. He climbed the thorn-tree too, scratching himself a good deal more on the way up than the river boy had done. Just as he got near the top, his shorts gave a doleful rip, and looking down he saw another of those nasty three-cornered rents his mother would sigh over. 'Oh dear, poor Mother, it's lucky she doesn't have to mend both our shorts.—*You* will have had a patch put on yours, next time I see you in a mirror—but she won't have had to trouble about that one—only mine. Perhaps it would make it seem less tiresome if she could think of it like that—two mends in one.' He pushed through the last thorns and stretched out a cautious neck into the blue sky.

The landscape was already changed from the view he had seen at the river-bank. He had noticed before how very quickly views altered in this land. Before one was expecting to see anything new, all the landmarks had vanished. So it was now. The purple-headed mountains had stolen very much closer, their green foothills ran down into the corn close by; and great outlandish rocks stood up here and there in the corn, with pinnacles and holes right through them, and the air smelt of mountain herbs: sage and thyme.

'Look,' whispered the boy. 'There she is!'

On a mountain meadow a short way up among the rocks, stood the most magnificent white horse. Its mane and tail hung down like waterfalls, foaming to the ground, its great back rippled and shone as it moved and turned its gentle, inquiring head towards them. The dark eyes burned with watchfulness. The boys slipped down out of the tree softly, so as not to alarm the great creature. Then the river boy with nimble fingers plaited a halter of straw, and he rubbed some grain free of chaff to take in his hand to offer.

'Will that halter be strong enough?' asked Nat doubtfully. It looked so very flimsy, to rein in that gigantic neck and royal head.

'Oh, she'll come, once it's over her head.'

ELEVEN

The Maze

So they made their way quietly to the rocks, along the last
yards of their narrow path.

'I suppose,' said Nat, 'the horse made the path as she went.'
'Yes.'

'She doesn't make much mark in the corn, does she, for so big
a creature!'

'No, and there are others who come this way. They go through
the corn, and it just closes again behind them and they leave no
trace at all.'

They scrambled up the rocks with as little clatter as they
could, clutching at tufts of wild thyme. They were not attempt-
ing to catch the great horse unawares, for her dark eyes followed
every movement; in fact she had probably watched their two
brown heads advancing through the corn for the past hour,
from her upland meadow. She showed no fear, but they did not
wish to startle her. As they drew nearer, something in her

appearance troubled Nat with a half-recognition. It was not that she looked *like* Rose; for she was at least twice as big and in the full vigour of her prime, and altogether more powerfully built— although not the least like a cart-horse. Nathaniel had never seen any animal with such clouds of rippling fine hair for mane and tail. Old Rose's mane had been sparse and irregular and tawny-white, like the last storm-bleached grass on a bog in January. This was a white that was *meant* to be white: not faded, but dazzlingly bright and as fine as his mother's hair. Yet in spite of all the differences between them, there was something which went on reminding him of the old mare. She held her royal head as Old Rose had done, tucked in a little to her breast, with neck arched. She pawed the ground with Rose's delicate impatience. And her great size and glory, though they did not belong to Rose herself, belonged to Nat's daydreams woven about her in the days when he used to lean on the gate and watch her drifting over the green hill with the magpies on her back. He had imagined the desert round her, boundless and bare, himself an Arab on her back, and in the distance the flying gazelle they would overtake before night fell.

For her part, too, the big horse was busy with intent thoughts of Nathaniel. She hardly glanced at the river boy, and it was to Nat that she came up softly and decidedly, and leaned her white velvet nose into his hand. With short warm puffs she searched round his brow and looked him all over. He fed her with a handful of the golden wheat, and took the halter and put it, rustling, over her head. She was too big for him to have reached if she had not herself bent her head right down. His heart danced with pride at her friendliness to him; and though he stood a little in awe of her, and though her great shoulders blazed so blinding white against the blue mountain sky that they seemed themselves like snowy shoulders of the mountains, he longed to be up on her back and riding her.

She swung her head round at his thought, as if he had spoken; and suddenly, like an avalanche, she sank to her knees.

'Can I *really* ride her?' whispered Nat. 'Does she mean me to get up?' The river boy smiled and nodded, so he waded through

the foam of mane that swept along the ground, and clambered
on to her back, taking a good handful of mane to hold on by.
Then there was such a heave of rippling neck that he was quite
smothered, and bumped his nose. He had forgotten that horses
get up forefeet first, unlike the awkward humble cows and sheep,
who stay kneeling in front while they poke up into the sky
behind.

Another heaving and earthquaking and the great horse was
up. Nathaniel seemed so high, he would not have been surprised
to find she had unfurled wings like Pegasus. But instead she
gave a violent shake that nearly brought him toppling down,
and then began to move her great legs that were like trees
walking. The river boy held the halter rope and led the way.
They moved along the grassy verge between the mountains and
the corn to a distant gate, where Nathaniel from his high seat
could see a wagon, tilted with its shafts towards the sky. It was
newly painted—kingfisher blue. Collar and harness, the brass
new-polished and twinkling, the leather shining, hung upon one
shaft, and in the collar sat the kingfisher himself, and his wife
and three young ones, all as like each other as five peas,
preening and spreading out their wings as if to match them
against the new paint.

'Why are they so far from the river—surely it's miles away by
now?'

'Not very far. It takes a loop our way (you can't see it in the
corn); and the kingfishers like the mountain streams as well.'
He pointed to a trickle that wound down among the rocks with
little falls, twisting a thread from one dry stone to another, until
it sank away in the corn at last.

'Where does that come from?' asked Nat.

'From snow-springs in the mountain-tops. A longer way off
than you would think. The clearness of the air deceives you.'

The kingfishers, at that, flew off in a string as if, even with
wings, there were no time to lose, and Nathaniel's eye soon lost
their flight over the corn, for they vanished among the tall blue
cornflowers. He had half a mind to wheel the great horse after
them, away and up into the mountains. But she would not heed

the pressure of his heel. For all his proud riding, it was the river boy with his halter whom she really obeyed, and he was urging her backwards now between the shafts. Nat jumped down and helped him lower them. Then they put the collar on her neck, and fixed it to the shafts and did up all the shiny straps and buckles. Nat wondered if they ought to plait her mane and tail, to keep them out of the way, but as soon as he laid doubtful fingers on her neck, she half-reared in the shafts and snorted with indignation, shaking it free. So he minded his own business and left her to manage her flowing tresses as best she liked. But seeing that she was still indignant with him and tossed her head whenever he came near, the boys went off to cut themselves two-pronged forks from the bushes by the gate. When they came back she whinnied.

The gate opened between posts that marked no boundary: they stood forlornly in the full tide of corn, without hedge or fence on either side. But beyond the gate a width of corn as broad as a river had been cut, and the sheaves had been bound and set up in stooks. This broad way stretched into the distance, growing smaller and smaller, until it reached a crest and sank out of sight.

The full heat of the day was lessening as they set to work. The river boy taught Nat how to pitch the sheaves and turn the spikes of his fork away from the loader's face: how to load a wagon so that the corn was not rubbed from the ear, and the load went up as straight as the sides of a house. When Nat was pitching, the work went slowly. He realized now why labourers in the fields at Bourne seemed half-asleep in the slow swing of their arms. Higher and higher rose the load, until he could not reach up with his sheaf to the river boy's downstretched arm, and it fell back on his own head. So then they turned the white mare round, and led her back to the gate, and built the foundations of a stack. Next time it was Nat's turn to load, and sheaves seemed to him to fly up in flocks from the river boy's fork, like great flustering golden hens. They bounced in on him so fast, he could hardly lay them quick enough to prevent himself from being buried up to the waist. When he gasped,

'Steady!' the boy would slacken speed; but he soon forgot, and began once more to send the sheaves flying up, keeping time to the beat of a lively jig which he was whistling. Nat was kept so busy, he had no time to look about him until he was so far above the back of the horse that even the river boy had hard work to pitch his sheaves so high, and the last ones came floating up more slowly. He tapered the top of his load, caught an upflung rope and laid it across, and the boy made it fast to the cart-tail.

Then the whole creaking, rustling mountain of corn swung round slowly, and Nat, balancing on top, with legs wide apart, had time to breathe and gaze about him. He could see from side to side across his country. The river flashed and wound between the golden acres, and the path of stooks stretched away like a second river. From his height he could see that it twisted ahead and doubled backwards and forwards over the slopes. It occurred to him that it looked like a maze he had seen once, with a sundial at its centre, in an old-fashioned garden.

What a queer way to reap, he thought, and what a labourer he must be, whoever he was, to reap this ever winding and unwinding path, that was yet so small among the limitless fields. If it followed more than a mere whim—if from a bird's-eye view the reaping traced some pattern—if it were indeed a maze— then would it not lead to some centre? Nathaniel could hear a lark, swallowed up in the blue afternoon. He wondered what the lark could see at the centre of the maze, and what he made of it in his endless song.

TWELVE

The Shadowless Farm

THE boys and the white horse finished their stack and began another one farther on. Looking back, they could see with pride a long, twisting sweep of bare stubble, and in the distance, the comfortable round stack by the gate, already as small as a beehive. Nat wondered how they had done so much in one afternoon. It was only now declining into evening, and he was not yet tired. He was proud of the new deftness of his pitching, and his nimbleness on the load; he felt he could go on for ever, up and down the gentle slopes, wherever the mysterious reaper led. It was partly the company of the white mare that made the work pass so pleasantly, though indeed there was nothing he had ever done with the river boy that he had not enjoyed. Yet the great fabulous white creature added something new to their companionship. With her gentleness and her great beauty she drew them even closer in contentment, and they took turns to guide her, and sometimes rode ʾto and fro from the stack standing on her back, to feel the huge muscles roll under their bare feet; and then they would shout and sing.

As they were beginning the second stack, Nat, going ahead to knock over the stooks, found under the shadow of one a large, flat-sided flask in a wicker cover, and a shallow straw basket covered with leaves. There was also a bucket of water—still shaking rings of ripples as if it had only just been set down.

'Are these for us?' he exclaimed; and the river boy nodded delightedly.

'Left on purpose.' He ducked his head into the bucket and came out streaming and refreshed, advising Nat to do the same. Then they carried the bucket to the mare to drink. They un-hitched her from the shafts, and she ambled about while they sat down in the shade under the cart. There they uncorked the bottle and took the leaves off the basket. The leaves were still fresh: they could not have been picked long.

But whoever had left these refreshments had come and gone invisibly. The basket was full of small mountain strawberries, and in the flask was cider, more delicious than any home-brewed at Bourne. As Nat drank, all the energy of early morning rushed back into his veins, his heart danced, and love of the midsummer corn and the white horse became almost a pain to him. He could not have enough of it, he longed to wake and sleep for ever with the white horse beside him and the gold corn in a ring about him. They sat in silence till, between them, they had finished the basketful, and then the horse came to see what they had, but preferred for herself the green leaves of the cover.

After this the work went on again, but Nathaniel had grown restless after drinking that wine. The cart moved far too slowly for him towards the heart of the corn: his longing to find the centre of the maze grew stronger and stronger. All the long day they had swept in vague circles, slowly narrowing in. But when he stood on the tip top of the second stack he thought he saw what he was looking for at last. The straight sides of the stack fell giddily away, down, down to the golden floor. It seemed to him he was as high above the cornland as the lark he had heard singing. He felt that the whole world lay spread below him.

The standing corn fell away abruptly to the west, and he could, from his dizzy vantage-point, look down directly into the vale below. What he saw might have been a mile from him as the crow flies, or rather as the lark descends, and heaven knows how much farther by the windings of the maze. A church-tower rose in the centre of a circle of roofs—the byres and barns and house and ricks of a farm. In the deceptive, crystal-clear air they looked almost near enough below for him to have thrown his pitchfork down upon the roof of the tower. He counted twelve roofs in all—like the figures of a clock, he thought. Or no, more like a sundial indeed, with the tower in the middle for the finger to cast the shadow. It was then that he realized with a strange, sharp surprise, that the tower cast no shadow at all. All round it beneath him the twelve roofs lay in the bright sunlight of evening, which was drawing from his own feet already so long and dark a shadow, stretching out far beyond the shadow of the stack. Yet the whole farm, and the ancient tower, and the flowering trees, lay in a circle of untroubled radiance. Gazing at them long and silently, Nathaniel felt as though something he had always minded had been put right, as though he had found something he did not know he had lost.

He looked a moment longer, to print on his memory—for ever, he thought—every detail of the farm, the tower, and the roofs bathed in shadowless light, promising hospitality; also the thick, dark trees, partly in white flower—myrtle perhaps, amongst the yews—that so closed it about. He could not be sure whether there was any gate into it, nor whether the tower belonged to a church: there was certainly no graveyard.

He slid off the stack then, saying no word of what he had seen. The river boy had been all this time on the cart below, from whose level he could not yet have had a glimpse of the tower. Nathaniel was possessed with longing to reach it, and feared, he did not know why, that he might be prevented. He had never wanted anything so much in his life. 'Not yet!' the river boy had cried, and had held him back, when with the same intense desire he had wanted to follow Old Rose through the door under the music-maker's waterfall. Would he say 'Not yet!' again? Nathaniel was not going to give him the chance. So he worked on for a while, until it was his turn again to go ahead and knock over the stooks. The moment a twist of the path had hidden him from sight, he threw down his fork and began to run.

He pelted as if the wind was under his heels, down the long slopes, up the hills, back and forth as the path doubled and zig-zagged and spiralled. The farm was hidden by the corn all the way, except for glimpses of the top of the tower, which told him he was circling round it as he ran, and it seemed to beckon to him. His heart began to pound painfully, his breath hurt. After all his running, was he really coming any nearer to his goal? Still he went on, at a jog now, and at last at a plod. His longing to be there grew fiercer as his strength failed. Hazy twilight had come, and a moon that had seemed to be a wisp of cloud all day was gathering a glimmer of light now, before she sank. Nathaniel rounded a bend like a hundred bends before, and stopped short —in dismay! The farm was in full view, only one shallow valley away, under the slopes of the mountains: the path of stooks ran straight ahead down the hill towards the mound beyond, on which it stood. But at the bottom of the hollow the stooks came to an end abruptly and the uncut corn rose all around— sweeping up the slope and encircling the farm itself in thick, whispering ranks no traveller might dare to trample.

Tears sprang into Nathaniel's eyes. He had never dreamed the maze itself might end before it reached the shadowless place of his desire. Now, only now, he remembered that he had seen no path leading up to the farm, and no gate.

The tower beckoned to him still, lit by the hazy yellow of the sunburnt moon, and the whole view swam and shone with his unshed tears of disappointment. As he blinked them away, he saw something curved and gleaming in a fallen swathe of poppies. It was the very same sickle he had seen hanging on the wall in the Mill; he was sure he recognized its old, scarred, razor-edged blade. And there, for proof, among the speedwell, rusty and furred all over with dew, stood the huge old hour-glass that had hung below it. Of the reaper there was no sign at all: he had flown. Nathaniel was filled with anger against him for stopping short, whoever he might be—until he reflected that perhaps the reaper too had longed to reach the farm, and could not get there before night fell. He seized the handle of the sickle with a wild idea of cutting his own way through, and swung the heavy blade with all his might. It whistled with a terrifying swish, the edge flashed by, the great weight of the blade dragging him round with it helplessly: so that sky and earth spun before his eyes, and it knocked with a dismal clang against the hour-glass.

The sickle fell from his frightened hands as the hour-glass rolled on its side. A cold shiver ran through all the corn, which suddenly blanched dead white with something more than the moonlight. From the shining farm came stealing a dying burst of the same haunting music that once before had called Nathaniel away. Far behind him he heard a cry, and turning, saw for a moment, on the skyline, the wagon tilted with empty shafts. Over the tops of the corn something white came floating —the wraith of a small white pony with a magpie on her back— and it flitted past him to the farm. Even as he watched, the tower and the roofs began to sink slowly out of sight. Whether they sank into the earth, or whether the corn spread wider round them, bearing Nathaniel farther and farther from the centre, he could not tell. The vision had gone, only the corn closed all about him, desolately whispering. For the first time, he wanted to be gone before he was taken away. Since the farm had vanished, he wanted nothing else. Kneeling by the hour-glass, he tugged at its heavy iron case until he succeeded in setting it upright, so that the full glass of sand began to run down into the emptied one.

Then he began deliberately to do the opposite of getting into his head. He remembered with an effort the branch he had been sitting on, in the beech-tree, and the feel of the branch he had torn off, in his hand. He said to himself: 'The branch is cold and wet at the back of my knees, my hand smarts, it's thundering.

Mr. Greenaway is shouting. It's pouring. I am going indoors.'
Then he opened his eyes again and jumped down and ran
through the rods of pouring rain that stood as thick as standing
corn. He ran into the kitchen at Bourne, shaking his wet hair
out of his eyes, for he was not quick enough to run between the
drops.

THIRTEEN

The Wrong Way Back

THAT return of his own accord from the river country marked a change in Nathaniel. Back at Bourne, he was for a long while restless and dissatisfied. His longing to reach the shadowless farm would not be stilled, though he was surprised and grieved to find how very soon his memory of it blurred. He soon could not remember any more the exact arrangement of the roofs, nor how tall the tower had been. Gradually it was all to fade from his mind, except the intense desire it had filled him with, and its look of promise and beckoning invitation. Some kind of life more brilliant and exciting than had ever been his went on, he was sure, under those roofs, behind those thick trees. He hardly knew whether he was sure he would never find it again, or sure he would one day reach it: his feelings were such a topsy-turvy mixture of despair and delight whenever he thought about it. But the days slipped by; Autumn came; wheat of a more commonplace kind was harvested at Bourne; and a sheet of wasps trembled over the fallen apples in the orchard, with a noise like a soft tambourine, never still. Still no call from the river came to him: no glimpse, not even in a dream.

He took to making maps of imaginary rivers, inventing

adventures for himself—a clash of armies at a ford, a princess he saved from drowning, a monster he fought—but always when he reached the mouth of the river and came to chalk in the blue sea, he would throw away the paper and dream and wish and wish. If he could not find the farm again, then could he not at least be on his way to the sea? Was he never to continue his journey?

He had always been able to be perfectly happy without obvious occupation—he used to go into the woods, not for a walk, not to fish or hunt or build houses or watch birds, so much as simply to *be* there. Once he had climbed the gate into the green stillness, he did whatever came into his head, or watched whatever came into sight; and if nothing special came into either, he might spend as much as half an hour at a time with no more stir or active thought than a tree—and just as enjoyably. If the boys at school had known of this they would have laughed at him, but he did not let them guess. For when he was in company he grew excited and talkative and nobody played noisier games than he.

But lately his hours by himself had begun for the first time to seem empty. Trying to keep still fidgeted him, and made his nose itch. Having watched a solitary bee disappear into her burrow on the hot hillside, he was no longer perfectly content to lie in the sun till she came backing out again. He teased her out with a straw, and then rummaged off the cover of turf and earth, and laid her whole burrow bare till he came on the grub in its glazed chamber at the end, with a crumb of yellow bee-bread as big as his little finger-nail. He took this back to his attic, and the sharp fragrance from this morsel, quintessence of honey-smell, filled his whole room. He made a labelled drawing of the burrow, marked Bee, Entrance, Tunnel and so on, till it bristled with information. He gave it to his mother. She admired it; but she asked what would become of the bee when she returned to her ravaged home?

He made endless plans of inventions. There was a car to be worked entirely by a series of small water-wheels, in a water-system that ran round inside. He abandoned that in favour of shoes made of orange peel which looked delightful to sew and would be so soft and pleasant to the foot. But that, too, came to nothing.

Finally he did invent a tape-measure that sprang back into its box by means of an elastic band stretched inside, and with the tape so fastened to it that it twisted the band up as it was pulled out. He decorated the box with gold patterns and presented it to his mother for her birthday. She was enchanted with it, but disappointed him by utterly refusing to have its workings explained. It worked like magic, she said, and so she wanted it to remain, springing mysteriously back into the slit with no more visible machinery than a lizard's tongue.

As she sat there pulling it out and letting it fly back, she suddenly asked Nathaniel if it were not growing rather dull for him at Bourne, with so few friends of his own age; and what would he think about going away to school? That was the first of many discussions and plans. Letters were written and uncles consulted; for Nat's answer, rather to his own surprise, had been Yes.—He would like to go. Sometimes he felt he had been silly to set all this afoot—how could he dream of leaving Bourne? But he was already, in another country, a traveller, and there he had learnt that he could not stay in one place for very long. Besides, there were the holidays. Besides, he wanted to learn things Miss Bone could not teach him. Besides, he wanted to see the world for himself.

All this time he never once visited the river. Had he, by deliberately willing his way home, broken some link with it? Yet, he reasoned, that might just as well work the other way round—if he could will his way from the river to Bourne, could he not will his way there again? Might not the river boy be waiting for him to do that very thing? Another part of Nat knew that this was not so, but he would no longer listen. He longed to force something to happen. He would *invent* a way to get there, as he had invented the tape-measure's spring.

The ways he tried were various. He crept down to the kitchen one night after everyone was asleep, and toasted Grandfather's favourite strong green cheese over the dying embers to give himself dreams. If he could dream, surely the current of his continual thoughts would carry him to the river? But the inadvisable meal only kept him awake in no very comfortable condition, watching the unhurrying stars pace by the window till dawn began. Then he fell asleep at last and dreamt, unhappily—of toasted cheese.

He tried getting into his head again, sitting still until he had pins and needles, and ached all over, but he had lost the art of that. He read the *Arabian Nights* and all other books of magic he could find for descriptions of spells, and tried as many as he had the materials for, but he could not put much faith in his own hocus-pocus; it was all a sham beside his real memories of the river. Only once did he begin to believe in what he was doing, and frightened himself. Afterwards he did dream of the river— if one could call the mere sound of laughter a dream. The Miller's laughter it was, shaking the steps of the Mill with hearty rumbles of mockery.

That was the night when Nat had crept out of the house in his pyjamas and had run three times round it widdershins in the fierce Autumn starlight. Then standing by the door with his hand on the old broken-beaked stone eagle, which had once been a pinnacle on a church tower, he actually said his prayers backwards as witches used to do. He had hardly said three words before horror came over him at what he was doing. He rushed upstairs and flung himself down by his bed and said his prayers properly; and then he got right under the bedclothes, half-frightened, half-ashamed, his ears burning. Nothing evil pounced down on him, and he fell asleep at once, only to have, in the small hours, that fleeting dream of mockery. This was the end of his attempts for some while, until midwinter came, and with it, one night, a deep fall of snow.

Next day he was just leaving for school with his sou'wester pulled down over his eyes, and at his back a haversack of ham sandwiches and apples and cake for his lunch, packed lugubriously by Mrs. Dill. She kept adding yet one more and one more package, stuffing them in while Nat stood impatiently beside the flames of the fresh-lit fire which flickered palely in the snow-light that filled the kitchen. Mrs. Dill was afraid of snow, and treated Nat as if he might die of cold and starvation before five o'clock. Or worse. Her imagination warmed to more and more dreadful possibilities as the fire burnt up higher in the range.

'Now don't you fall down in the snow and knock your head and cut it open, Master Nat. Nor don't you go to sleep in the snow. *Those that go to sleep in the snow don't wake up in this world!*'

At that, a plan came into Nathaniel's head, the most fool-hardy he had ever devised. As he went out into the mysterious, muffled brightness of the snow-drifts, he muttered to himself, 'Now I *will* get back to the river, so there! We'll see who laughs last today.'

As he trudged through snow that came half-way up his black rubber boots, even in the windswept places, the sky clouded over once more and it began to fall again. The twinkling, myriad flakes showed dark against the sky, his footsteps filled up behind him, and the gate he had opened with a jolt, and the brambles he had brushed bare, were rebuilt at once into bars and arches of snow. He planned to make two great snow lions to sit crouching on each side of the front door. He would stick electric torches in their heads for eyes, and terrify Mrs. Dill when she locked up after tea.

'But *that*,' he nodded to himself, 'will be *afterwards*. When I come home!' He did not mean home from school, but from a longer expedition.

He got through the long day inattentively. His eyes kept straying to the window where the flakes still sifted, drifted, eddied down. How would the river look, dark between magically whitened fields and mountains?

When four struck, he slipped away from the cheerful crowd of snowballers. He heard the voices of Jim and Phil and Freddy calling him faintly when they realized he was gone, but he was already speeding down the hill in the opposite direction to Bourne. The snowfall had paused again; the sun showed through a rift before it set—a dull globe of crimson. It was difficult to believe the ebbing daylight came from that, and not the snow

itself; the sun seemed nothing but a painted ball. Yet the church
tower, when he looked back, had a rosy face for a moment before
it faded to a pinched blue. Looking away again, Nat saw that
the sun had gone, and night came flying over the empty
hills.

He made his way over a piece of wild and desolate moor he
had seldom visited, slipping as he went on bog-pools whose
wicked black ice was hidden by the snow, and bumping into
great round stooping bushes of gorse, with sharp prickles hidden
under their white cloaks. In the middle of the moor was a dis-
used quarry half-filled with snow, and when he slithered down
into its speckless counterpane he was tired out indeed, and so
hot that the warmth from his neck beat up under his chin like
sunlight. He stood for a moment in the silence, half-inclined to
listen to thoughts he had not heeded before. He thought of his
mother's anxiety when he did not return to tea, and of the
comforting brightness of the wood fire in Grandfather's room.

'Well, I can't turn back *now*!' he said—aloud, to make it
more convincing. 'And anyhow, once I get to the river I need
not stay long—only just to prove I can!'

From the twigs of a thorn in the dusk above his head, a
frozen sparrow, which had clung to its perch while strength
lasted, slipped down and fell into the snow, as if dislodged by
the stir of Nathaniel's voice. It lay on its back, stiff with cold, its
curled toes drawn up on its narrow breast. He picked it up and
ruffled its soft feathers, marvelling at the tiny ones that rayed
round the filmy eyelid. He shivered a little and yawned, and
putting the bird into the top of his jersey in case it might
recover, he curled up in the snow himself, his head on his
haversack, and started obstinately to count sheep—sheep with
fleeces of snow who jumped through a gap beside a dark river.
He did not intend to 'wake up in this world.'

In the thorn-tree a dumpy knob screwed its head round to
look at him and hooted something into his drowsy ears that
sounded like: 'Too *wit*less boy! Too *fool*ish boy!' But numbing
sleep was creeping into Nat's bones, along with the creeping
cold. The little owl shook its feathers—spat out a pellet of

mouse-fur to express its feelings—but settled down again to keep watch, ruffled up against the cold and glaring about it uneasily.

At last the chimes of half-past five stole across the clear, silent air to Rough, as he still sat patiently by the gate, waiting for the far-off shaking of the earth that should long ago have told him Nat was nearly home. He had been growing more and more uneasy as it grew later and darker, and now, with a whine, he pricked his ears once or twice uncertainly, and then started off on the way to the village, snuffing for Nathaniel's vanished footprints as he loped along.

Presently Miss Bone heard a scuffling at her door, and when she opened it, Rough bounded in indignantly, as if he suspected her of keeping Nathaniel in. He insisted on searching the house thoroughly, though she very much objected to his snowy paws, especially upstairs, and went after him with a duster, mopping up as fast as he thawed. Only when he had looked in the coal-cellar *and* her hat-box, was he finally convinced that Nat was not there—and then he was as eager to be off again as he had been to come in. Out in the starlit village street he paused, sniffing the air, and then suddenly set off again as if in answer to a call, though there was no sound at all except the muffled indoor noises of the cottages, and the faint ticking and tinkling of ice forming in the ditch. Away, away he sped—over the snow towards the moor. He floundered through the drifts, his tail jingling with icicles, till at last his kindly, shaggy face was hanging over the edge of the little quarry, looking down at a huddled shape, half-sunk into the snow. He leapt down, barking, and rushed to Nathaniel, and licked his face and pawed at his arm—but he could not awake him.

So it was that Miss Bone, having set her house to rights again at last, was a second time disturbed, and this time Rough fairly twirled her out into the starlight by the hem of her mauve serge skirt. He was behaving so oddly that she put on a pair of stout boots and called out the blacksmith, next door, with his lantern, and let Rough lead them wherever he pleased. He flounced ahead, barking with impatience.

Nathaniel at last opened his eyes drowsily, to a horrible

aching and stiffness, a black cold where lanterns danced and voices scolded and exclaimed with relief, and he was carried home in the blacksmith's arms, his teeth chattering, and shaking all over. He was too chilled and dazed to explain himself at all as they put him to bed with hot bottles by a fire. He was only dimly aware of Mrs. Dill, busy with blankets in the firelight, tears on her cheeks—too overcome by a real disaster to make any gloomy prophecies at all.

And of his foolhardy sleep all he remembered was a confused idea of rushing icy darkness, a torrent of darkness bearing him away and away—and a sense of having lost something, by his own fault, which perhaps would never be found again.

FOURTEEN
The Aqueduct

L YING in his mother's big bed, aching and throbbing, Nathaniel began to be ill of a fever. After feeling so cold that he felt he would never be warm again, he began now to feel on fire, and tossed about, restlessly muttering, 'Lost . . . lost', and talking lightheadedly about a river. His mother bent over him from time to time: then she would sigh and sit down again in her armchair by the fire, and listen to the snow hissing in the chimney.

When midnight tolled out, very clear across the empty fields, suddenly Nathaniel sat up with a start, his hand in the neck of his pyjamas, and cried out wildly, 'The sparrow! Where's the sparrow?' Then he sank back as if at last he was falling asleep.

But in that moment, unwillingly now—afraid to leave the firelit room—afraid to leave his mother—he began, after all, to go back to the river. It seemed to draw him as a stick is drawn by the current, eddying and drifting, though he clutched at the sheet and muttered, 'No, no! Not now—not now!' He was afraid to go, for the fear that he had somehow lost the river boy for ever lay like a small cold weight at his throat where the frozen sparrow had lain. But he was drifting there, he could not help himself.

In a little while all fell still and he came to himself standing in a desolate and starry wilderness—a forest, beyond whose tops rose up the dark sides of a great ravine, shutting in the sky. He had a sense of being very deep down. On one side of the ravine, out of the cloudless sky of unwinking stars, he could see falling an endless, terrible cascade of snow. Relentlessly, hopelessly, without a sound, it fell from the lips of the crag like a river— like spray, crumbling and turned into flakes of snow by the deathly cold air as it floated down.

It *was* a river: he could see the gleam of the brim of the water as it toppled over the edge of the chasm. With a smart of fear, he thought, 'That's my river! It's my fault!' But what could be the meaning of this cold underworld, this dreadful rift in the happy valley, where his river was wasting away in falling snow? The trees round him at the bottom of the ravine were ancient, and yet he felt that the abyss was somehow of his making—that it would never have opened had it not been for his obstinacy.

He felt a stifling panic—he *must* get out, he must, he must! He took a step or two into the tangled frosty darkness of the forest, and almost at once stumbled over something which he thought was a low boulder. He stooped to look at it and saw at his feet— the river boy! He was lying as though fast asleep, his head on a haversack, just as he himself had lain in the quarry. Nat bent down and shook his snow-powdered shoulder, but the boy would not wake. For a terrible moment he thought he was dead, stiff and cold, and that he himself was the only creature alive in the ravine. Then—apparently—the boy chirruped! At any rate there *was* a chirp, and it came from the boy's throat! There was a rustle in his jersey, a struggle—and out thrust a ruffled head with beady eyes. A sparrow, perfectly warm and revived, sprang out and flew away into the undergrowth, soft and low, as little birds do when disturbed at night.

It gave Nat back his courage. If the bird had grown warm inside his jersey, the boy could not be dead. And in the direction of its flight, he thought he saw a winking light. He put up his hands round his mouth and hallooed with all his might. Then the light appeared again, creeping and wavering about between the trees, moving more or less towards him, but slowly, with many pauses, and by roundabout ways. Presently he saw that it was a lantern, fastened to a stick on the roof of a queer, rickety handcart, drawn by a tall old woman. She stumped along slowly in spite of his urgent calls, and stopped now and then to poke about in the bushes, and once she seemed on the point of going to sleep where she stood, nodding between the handles of the cart. He ran up to her and pulled at her long, fur cloak. It felt as if it were made of all kinds of different skins—long pelts and short, sewn together haphazard. He explained breathlessly what was the matter. She did not appear to be listening to what he said. She only looked piercingly at him out of her long dark face, with eyes so deep sunk he could hardly see them at all. But she nodded, though she did not speak. He felt immensely comforted by her presence, though a little afraid of her: she looked a stern old woman, and was so very tall, over six foot she must be, though bent. She poked the river boy indifferently, then turned her back and began breaking off sticks for a fire. Nat helped her eagerly, often glancing at the face of the river boy, fast-shut in sleep. It wore something of the same strange expression he had seen on it once before, the night the boy danced on the water. What was he dreaming of now? Perhaps of a bed-room in firelight, where a mother was sitting in her chair, watching out the night, and listening to the snowflakes hissing in the chimney.

When the fire was blazing—casting a red glow high up into the great moss-hung boughs—the old woman drew out from her cloak, still without one word, a handful of chestnuts, split them across with a knife and laid them round the fire. Then she took a black pot from the handcart and hung it over the flames to heat. The handcart bristled with handles of tools of all shapes and sizes, and while she waited for the pot to boil, and the chestnuts to roast—sitting round the fire in their polished skins like a row of patient beetles—she roved to and fro, poking and snipping and shaking off snow and listening at the trunks of trees. Dumb she might be, but she evidently had very sharp ears—for her head was turned to the northern skies, long before Nat heard the murmur of approaching wings. They made a soughing like the tone of a big harp, growing louder and louder. He was staring up at the Milky Way, and he saw the stars one by one blotted out for an instant, as a flight of great birds passed overhead, migrating southwards.

They passed on. But one left the invisible flock, circling lower and lower, and presently glissaded down with a great rush and thunder of wings through the snowy tree-tops, and came to rest beside the fire. It was a great swan, dragging one black foot in the snow and couching his beak wearily on his heaving breast. The gaunt old woman went to him, examined the hurt leg, and burrowing in her handcart for ointment and instruments, she smeared the damaged joint and bound it up in a splint. The swan stood very meekly while she did so, and settled down by the fire waggling his tail like a contented goose. But he looked at Nathaniel out of the corner of his eye, very haughtily, before he put his head behind his wing and went to sleep.

The old woman still took no notice of the river boy. She hardly seemed to know he was there, and indeed he looked so fragile, almost transparent in the mingled snow-light and star-light, that he might have been only a shadow on the ground. The woman poured out broth into a wooden bowl for Nat. He was very glad of its warmth, though privately he thought the flavour unpleasantly like medicine. It smelt of fungi and withered winter berries and mouldering seeds. But he supposed that an old woman who was accustomed to wander the forest in the depths of a midwinter night could not be particular. The chestnuts were more appetizing—but he wished the river boy were sharing them with him. If only the boy were well, this great, whispering, shadowy place would be exciting, not frightening, and the chasm would not fill him with vague terrors of being in a trap. The river boy would have known the way out. But he only stirred and muttered in his sleep, with flushed cheeks, and Nat was very miserable to see him so. They seemed to have changed places: the boy was ill of the fever which should have been Nat's alone. And the shadows crept about his sleeping hands as if they would draw him away to be one of them, and wake no more.

Restless and silent, the woman began to collect armfuls of dead bracken and made a little shelter over the river boy, and presently beckoned Nathaniel to curl up inside there as well; and she leaned down and put her own cloak of patched skins over them both. He was very sleepy now himself, but before his eyes shut tight he thought for a moment, when she went back to the fire without her cloak, that he saw her wearing a gown as green as a leaf, with a hem as red and blue and gold as a June border. And for a moment she seemed to throw off her stoop and stand up as tall as a young tree. But perhaps it was only a chance effect of the firelight and the shadows.

He woke with the dusk of daybreak creeping into the little hut of bracken. The boy by his side had gone. Outside, the fire was still burning, fresh twigs crackled on it; and in the distance he heard a tapping. It seemed to him he had been dimly aware of noises—tapping and stirring and pacing about, and the creak of wheels—all night in his sleep. He jumped up and followed through the forest the tracks of two spindly wheels and a pair of clogs, till he came again on the old woman in a clearing, muffled up once more from head to foot in her furs. The old handcart was greenish in the dim morning light, and its threadbare hood was as thin as a winter leaf. The woman must have carried the river boy on her back, or stuffed him in among the calipers and spades and hammers; for he was lying as before, his flushed cheek on his arm, beside her.

She was kneeling by a pile of newly dug black soil, separating with extreme delicacy and care the finest filaments at the end of a root of a beech-tree. She bent and pushed and poked and rearranged, and then covered it all up with earth as before. The lame swan was standing a little less awkwardly this morning, and looking contentedly at his healing joint. One or two other creatures had joined the party—a curlew with a trailing wing, and a mouse who seemed to have toothache, for he sat up on one handle of the cart, nursing his swollen cheek in his paws. Silently, the woman handed Nathaniel three flat black biscuits for his breakfast, and then took no further notice of him, after the one piercing look, both stern and kind, that she gave to each of her patients. The biscuits tasted bitter, like bark, and he broke off an icicle and sucked it, to take away the taste and quench his thirst.

All that day he patiently helped the strange woman, wandering through the shadowy forest, pulling the cart while she carried the river boy in her arms. He believed that she would help them in her own time, even though she hardly seemed to care or know that they were there. She was an oddly contradictory person; for she would spend a great while skilfully coaxing the head of a smothered young oak into the light, and then just as carefully would wind a strand of ivy round its throat, which would choke it before it ever grew into a forest tree. She was always dropping her tools, too—they left a little trail behind them of tweezers, files, forks, tiny delicate scalpels and great hooks and grapples. At first Nathaniel picked them all up as they fell and put them back on the cart, but as she never seemed to mind whether he did or not, and as the cart was always full and bristling like a pin-cushion in all directions, he gave up bothering.

He loved to watch the old woman's long, gentle, ingenious fingers busy at the delicate tattered edge of a toadstool, or scooping out a hole in a stump, or filing smooth the edge of a stone. All the while, although she was drowsy and seemed to wander about in whatever direction took her fancy, they were actually moving quite steadily towards that point at the side of the ravine where the river fell in a tall cloud of snow through the grey air.

As once more evening drew in, they stood at the foot of the fall itself, under a great mound of snow that had piled up at its base. In all this desolate under-country there was no sound at all except, as they drew nearer, the soft roar and thud of this growing mound. It was almost a pillar now, rising dizzily above the heads of the trees.

This time, to shelter the boys and the sick creatures, the woman carved out a niche of snow in the base of the pillar; and the swan obligingly spread out his large downy wings over them all. The firelight shone on the white snow walls and roof, and the old woman's shadow moved to and fro outside, still busy, still nodding with sleep. Nathaniel took the river boy's hand in his, determined to hold it fast in his sleep, in case the woman might move off again in the night, and perhaps leave him so far behind that he could never again catch up with her and the boy.

All through his dreams he seemed to hear an endless hammering and hammering—echoing, regular blows of steel on stone, like a pulse beating. In the small hours he woke up. All was still—it was the silence that woke him. Even the sifting of the snow had stopped. The swan had vanished, and so had the boy and the curlew and the mouse. The fire was out. Had he been deserted?

Yet, as the light of a new moon filtered in through the doorway of the snow cave, he had a strange feeling of something standing over him, something huge, waiting. He crept out to see what it was, and found — bestriding the forest with arch upon arch, and spanning with its faint shadow acres of tree-tops—a great stone aqueduct, flung across from one side of the ravine to the other. He could hardly believe that he had not merely stepped from one dream into another; all Solomon's temple workmen could not have built so great a structure in a single night! As if to contradict this very notion, a last triumphant tattoo of hammer-blows echoed from the arch above, and immediately afterwards there was a scatter of tools, bouncing down among the branches. Above the edge of the parapet, against the thinning night, he thought he saw the hood of the little handcart bobbing along the aqueduct. No more snow fell. The aqueduct was built to the very crag where the river's lip had been. But when he put his ear against the nearest stone pillar, he felt, rather than heard, a murmuring thrill like running water, coursing far above his head. Then he heard a splashing too, the sound of a swan's huge wings beating the water for joy. Where was the river boy?

He called and called, but his voice sounded weak in the wintry air. Then, by chance, he stepped under the arch as he called again. Here his voice boomed: 'Are you up there?' And 'Up . . . here . . .' hallooed the echo faintly—but the echo had a hint of a familiar mockery.

'Come down!' shouted Nat joyfully. 'I can't climb up there!' But 'I'm . . . up . . . here,' mocked the echo unhelpfully.

'Very well—I'll meet you,' shouted Nat, for whom the wilderness now held no more terrors. And '. . . meet you' floated down.

By the gathering light of daybreak and the dwindling light of the moon, Nat could see that the farther side of the ravine was not so steep as this one. He plunged bravely into the forest and ran from arch to arch, calling to the floating echo above, till at last he reached the farther side and began to climb a narrow track. By hairpin bends it led him towards the top of the aqueduct and the plains above. As he panted up, clinging to rocks, too dizzy to look down, he thought he saw traces of chisel-marks and pick and shovel along the way, and once he found the helve of an axe, broken in two. At his heels a white morning mist began to rise, creeping up and up, covering the forest below and filling the chasm, hiding it away from his eyes for ever.

As the sun came up over the edge of the parapet, the head and shoulders of the river boy appeared beside it; and beside the boy's smiling face showed the haughty bead-black eye of the swan.

All phantoms and shadows of fear faded away under the mist below, and Nat laughed for joy. He struggled up in a cloud of his own breath in the keen air.

'Come on, sleepy-head, slow-bones,' the boy teased the panting climber: 'You haven't even *washed!*'

At that, just as he reached the top, the swan stood up and beat his wings and flung a fan of gleaming river-water full upon Nat's upturned face.

He shut his eyes tight—and opened them in his mother's bedroom, looking up into hers. The morning sun was shining.

'Well,' she said, 'how nice to see you look as if you knew me again! And your pulse has stopped hammering at last!' Nat smiled and wrinkled his nose at her, and made no answer. He was too happy for words. He had had a glimpse, before he was spirited away, of the river pouring out of the aqueduct, and streaming on through the sparkling plains of its own dear valley, and of the river boy riding a great swan, his arm round its neck.

FIFTEEN
The Town of Chimes

CHRISTMAS had gone by before Nathaniel had fully recovered his strength. During the first days of his convalescence, while he lay in the weak Winter sunlight, or listened to the soft rain that took away the snow, he was often by the river, though only for a few moments at a time. The two worlds seemed very close, and he was never for long unaware of them both, existing side by side. He would lie watching the sunlight cast up on the ceiling by the oval looking-glass on his mother's dressing-table, and while he idly gazed, the light would alter into a rippling net of shimmers—the reflection that flowing water throws up on the stones of a bridge. The room seemed always to be full of the delicious smell peculiar to the river; and when his mother read aloud to him, the undertones of her low voice were mixed with the indistinct talk of running water, and sometimes a faint echo of the mill-wheel turning. Then Nat could feel that just behind his pillow, so long as he did not turn his head, the river boy sat listening too. In the evenings, sitting by the fire of ash logs which Mr. Greenaway brought in—with his leathery face squeezed up into a hundred wrinkles of pleasure, to see Nat so much better—his mother would sometimes sing to him: old songs like 'The Ash Grove', and 'Oh the Briery Bush', and 'Under this Stone Lies Gabriel John'. When he was half asleep her voice seemed to fade and blend with another one—or was it only a memory?—and the thready twangle of a little harp brushed the air faintly, picking out the melody.

Birds, too, knocked against the window now and then, and on Christmas Eve Nathaniel's mother, standing at the window, suddenly cried out, 'Oh, Nat! If *only* you had seen—I do believe it was a kingfisher! It must have thought the window was a waterfall!'

But Nat *had* seen it—for only a moment before, drowsing on the borders of sleep, he had slipped into a meadow, where he watched the kingfisher flying in and out of a waterfall, while the river boy hopped across the river from one stone to another, teasing him to follow.

Next day he came downstairs for the first time, and it was as happy a Christmas as any he could remember. The weeks slipped by, and the withered Kissing Bough and holly wreaths had been burnt on the bonfire, and Nat was beginning to look out for the first snowdrops, when a new trunk and playbox were set out on the floor of his attic, and their gaping maws were fed with neat slabs of new, folded clothes. The beloved torn leather jacket, and the cap that had held such a multitude of treasures so usefully, were not to find a place there. These were school clothes. Nat, looking nervously in at them all, felt he would need a new skin as well—and a tougher one. The thought of the long journey and new life was partly exhilarating, partly alarming. On the whole he was glad to be going, more curious to know what it would be like than depressed at leaving Bourne.

He had a feeling that in some way or other he would reach

the end of his secret journey before he set off for school. In one
of those fleeting visits to the river while he was getting better, he
had seen a flock of herring-gulls fishing in a pool. It could not,
surely, be very far to the sea? But as he fully recovered, so the
two worlds drew apart again, and he lived wholly in the every-
day one. Thoughts of school seemed to widen the gap between.

At length came the very last day. The trunk and play-box
were strapped up, his room was unnaturally tidy, and Mrs. Dill
was brooding, as she went about her work, on the perils of
journeys. Nathaniel himself went from place to place saying
farewell to all his favourite haunts. In his pocket he carried his
precious crystal ball as a farewell present to the river boy, if he
should by any chance find him in time. Mrs. Dill had given it to
him for a birthday present two years ago. She said that, when
gazed into rightly, it would show the future, but she could not
teach him how to do it.

It was a treasure, and hard to part with, but he could think
of nothing else the river boy would like so well, and he felt, too,
on the edge of a life so new that when he returned—who could
say?—everything might be different. Something told him he
might not care for his old treasures so much.

The last place he visited was the same empty valley which
had once disclosed the flowery upper reaches of the river. He
had lost hope now of a final visit to the river, but all the same he
sat down on a log, his chin on his hand, remembering that first
day. Then, for luck, he had a last look in the crystal ball,
determining to leave it as near as he could remember to the spot
where the secret country had first opened. He hoped that the
river boy, passing that way alone, about his mysterious con-
cerns, might find it and guess who had left if for him.

When he looked into the ball, clouds were passing over it,
reflected from the sky, he supposed. But presently as his gaze
became more fixed, the clouds parted, and showed, as if from a
star's-eye view, minute and far away—but crystal-clear—the
whole course of the river. Brightest light streamed over it,
hiding the source, but he could see the nut-bushes where he had

first played with the river boy, and the slopes full of little
waterfalls. Perhaps beside one of them was still turning, too
small to be seen, the tiny water-wheel which the boy had made
him so long, long ago. Lower down, he saw dimly a deep-
sunken, shadowy hollow, round which the steep woods hung
closely. He saw the path to the mill-pool, and the Mill and its
wheel, and the flat-bottomed boat marooned under the weir.
He saw the island, he saw the limitless cornfields and a part of
the maze; but not the farm—oh, not the shadowless farm itself!
He saw a rolling band of mist that might have hidden the forest
in the chasm. He thought he saw through it the top of the
aqueduct, but was not sure. The river flowed on, winding away
by wood and pasture, hill and valley, moor and marsh.
Farther still, he saw a white road come down to the brink and
wind on beside the bank to a little town encircled with bare
willows, all fiery in the sun. Mysteriously, the town seemed to
lie across the river itself, and just behind it the mountains that
had marched on each side of the valley closed in across its end.
The view enlarged and came nearer. The crystal ball grew and
grew. It became the sky itself, and Nathaniel was inside, his feet
upon the dusty white road leading towards the city. He stood
still for a moment, drawing a deep breath of joy to be there at
last, once again. The water-cluck and sighing of reeds filled his
ears. Across the brown, swift, wintry current, a heron on the
opposite shore regarded him solemnly, balancing his huge beak
carefully and holding his tail as much out of the water as he
could. Then he looked sidelong, watching someone else,
farther downstream.

It was the river boy, just ahead, wagging his bare feet in the
water, the kingfisher on his shoulder. He was, as usual, expecting
Nat, and greeted him lightly, without any questions or any
account of himself. They strolled on together in the bright, cold
afternoon sunshine, towards the flashing windows of the little
town behind the willows.

'Is it on an island, partly?' asked Nat.

'No, it's built on the river itself—on piles and bridges,
perhaps. Some say all of it is floating really, though it seems

quite solid. All the streets are waterways.'

The fiery willows were full of golden tufts and balls, and as they drew nearer, Nat saw that these were mistletoe. On the pale berries were feeding a hundred thrushes, who sang as they feasted, till their song echoed from the city walls.

Inside the ring of trees, the river divided into half a dozen winding alleyways and water-lanes. To every tree were tied clusters of rafts; yet there seemed to be no one about. So the boys chose one at random, took a paddle from a heap, and worked their way along a narrow water-street into the heart of the town.

Tall, ancient houses leant over the water, or straddled right across the way, so that they paddled through tunnels underneath them. Some were built out so far that their greenish bow-windows spied in upon each other, close enough for a hand-shake between opposite neighbours. The very bridges all seemed to be full of rooms and galleries.

The raft floated on into a wide, main thoroughfare where marble palaces looked down at their reflections. They came out at length into the huge central square, a sheet of water sprinkled with elaborate fountains. From the great stone pedestals of these, rose up sheaves and spouts and arches and fans of spray in all directions, spilling out of stone shells, jetting from carved and twisted horns, blown by mermaids and tritons, and spurting from the nostrils of dolphins and sea-serpents. And all this tumult fell back again into marble basins surrounded by the still water of the river-square.

Round the basins were bollards and rings to moor one's vessel to, though the boys' raft appeared to be the only one abroad. All about stood stately buildings: towers and spires and domes and pinnacles. Could they all really be floating on the river?

The boy tied up the raft in the shadow of what seemed to be a cathedral, and sat playing with the kingfisher while Nathaniel went off alone to explore. The little town seemed utterly deserted. Sunlight streamed in at open window and door, but all was so silent that the ticking of clocks was the only sound to be heard besides the splashing of the fountains.

Growing bold, Nat tiptoed in through a palace gateway between the unwinking marble dragons, and crossed the sunlit courtyard and skirted the water-court beyond, and wandered down a cool colonnade into a ballroom.

White candles stood ready in all the huge crystal chandeliers, that were each as big as a hanging Christmas-tree; and fresh flowers were in the vases; and the floor was waxed and polished for the dancers' feet. Through arches beyond, he could see a banqueting hall, set for a feast, row upon row of gold and silver plate, glittering down the long tables. In the gallery above, music-scores stood open ready on the music-stands, violin and viola were propped against the stools, and the harpsichord was open, showing a flight of enamelled kingfishers on its keyboard lid.

But not a guest, not the ghost of a footman trod the floors.

Nat climbed up into the gallery and from there into a bell-turret, and looked down. Far below, the river boy lay asleep in the sun, and a spark of blue was darting in and out of a rainbow caught in the spray of the central fountain. Cupping his hands, he shouted down, 'Ahoy! Ahoy!' And all the empty walls swung back the echo: '. . . . oy . . . oy . . . oy . . .'

No other sound at all but the fountains splashing, the clocks ticking, the birds at their feast. The boy by the fountain still slept on. Long after, from the green mountain-side itself came back, thinner, fainter still, another echo '. . . oy . . . oy . . .'

Then Nathaniel, turning at a slight grating sound behind his head, noticed for the first time a huge striker, upright by the rim of the big bell which hung just above his head. It began to draw back, slowly and jerkily, raising its head to strike the bell, which was humming very softly with the last vibrations of Nat's voice. It seemed almost as though his shout alone had started the ancient machinery moving. Back and back it drew, quivering, and then suddenly: 'Dong!' it fell forward on the bell, with a note so profound and resonant that Nat felt he was hearing it in the pit of his stomach, not in his ears.

'Dong! . . . Dong! . . . Dong!' the bells in the cathedral

opposite followed suit, answering from all four of its belfries, North, South, East, and West; and all the other steeples began to chime. Clocks in all the old houses began to whirr and strike, with coppery voices and silvery, golden, brassy, iron, twangling and booming, playing carillons and tunes. Cuckoo-clocks cuckooed, grandfathers wheezed, alarms and fob-watches buzzed and ting-tingled. One clock-maker's shop-window that looked on the square fairly rattled with the commotion behind it. Nat suddenly wondered if it was at this shop that the Miller had bought his time-keeping landscape—for this surely was the town painted at moonrise, with the real clock-face set in the painted tower of the cathedral.

All the clocks were striking different hours. The only thing they agreed upon was that the time had come to strike something.

Nobody appeared, in spite of this busy reminder that time was flying. Yet suddenly—Nat blinked with astonishment to see it—the pavements all round the square were strewn with green leaves, and garlands were looped along from window to window over all the walls! He was positive they had not been there before the clocks struck. And now, too, banners were everywhere flowing out like smoke, unfurling from every tower. What procession, what coronation or triumph was about to begin?

SIXTEEN

Journey's End

THAT which did come through the garlanded and waiting city, down one of the main waterways and into the wide water-square, was as silent and as empty as the town itself. And no procession followed it.

It was a little ship: sail spread and full, though no wind blew—her ropes coiled and ready—great roses tied along her rail and prow. No one steered her, no one rowed or trimmed the sail; she swam like a swan through the glittering square, entered a farther street, and as silently vanished, her mast showing once or twice over the lower roof-tops.

Nathaniel let out the breath he had held, in a sigh. Then he turned and ran. Down the spiral stair, clatter, clatter, along the gallery, down again, across the enormous ballroom, flitting out through sun and shade into the square, then round by the pavement and into the street down which the ship had vanished. He pelted through the sleeping city, hearing far behind him the river boy's following feet and the whistle of the kingfisher—even the bird was outstripped and left behind.

At the end of the waterway, at the farthest gates of the city, beyond the willow-trees, loomed the vast arch of a cavern that led into the mountain-side. And into this the river flowed on, out of sight. As Nat darted in and along the narrow ledge of rock that ran beside the water, his footsteps filled the whole hollow of rock with whispering echoes. Farther and farther behind him through the darkness sounded the river boy's fading voice.

'Good-bye!' it called. 'Good-bye! Good-bye . . .' and the cavern shuttled to and fro the murmurs 'Aye . . . aye . . . I . . . I . . . I.' But Nat never slackened speed. All his heart was set upon the ship—his ship.

Presently the winding darkness of the cavern lightened, a circle of light showed, and grew larger. A moment more and Nat was out of it in the open air again. But how different an air! The inner side of the mountain had been still as the depths of a crystal ball: on this side it was a wild, hurrying, sparkling air which beat boisterously at his face. There was the taste of salt on his lips.

Before his feet lay the sea!

He stood and stared and stared. After the green valleys of the river, sheltered by their mountains, dreaming in a silence unbroken except by the birds or the wind in the leaves or the river over the stones, this wilderness of waves stretching on for ever and ever was lonely and terrible in its beauty. A traveller might sail across it, but when he had passed by, not a sign would be left to show that he had ever been there.

Crags on either side, black and sharp as fangs, ran down the steep mountain into the blue water that heaved at high tide. Foam was breaking close under the lip of the rock where Nathaniel stood, and the waves plunged on and rolled into caverns under his feet. He could hear their deep, booming voices, stern and fierce, answering one another through the quivering rock, and sometimes as the waves rushed in and drew out again, the air was blown up through a crack in a great gust and then sucked in again, as if a chained monster were breathing underneath. When he lifted his eyes, the dancing waves spread away boundlessly, mingling with the sky itself, for he could not see where sea and sky divided.

The breakers came sidling in with smooth, arched backs, close upon one another, till the foam began to creep along their necks and they thundered over at Nat's feet and drew back, grinding and roaring, down the shingle, drawing with them the last waters of the river's mouth.

Then Nathaniel, seeing the pure water mix with the salt, and be quite lost in it, grew suddenly afraid and turned back to look for his companion.

Surely the mountain-side had risen less steeply a moment ago? Surely he had not walked more than a step or two from the cavern's mouth? Yet now a great slab of rock rose between him and the lip of the cave, and over it the river fell like fine hair, in several long cascades, blowing in the wind. The crag beetled out, overhanging the place where he stood; he could not even look back into the cavern along the way he had come.

There was no return into that inner country—nor was there any way out from it to where he now stood on the brink of the sea. He could never now answer the river boy's good-bye. Since there was no help for it, he turned back again, between excitement and alarm, to face the ocean.

And there, so close under the rocks to leeward that he had not seen it at first, rocking on the mingled currents where the river flowed into the waves, was the ship, waiting, her prow pointing out to sea. The sun was going down at the end of a shining path, but soon there would be stars to steer by.

He looked up, waiting for the Pole Star, the pilot star for mariners, to prick through the thickening dusk. While he stared overhead, it seemed that the surf grew suddenly quieter, more like the soughing of the evening wind in the silver firs at the bottom of Bourne Wood, and the creak of the little ship's tackle grew more like the cry of the wood gate, straining at its latch in the gusts. When he thought he had found his star, he looked down once more. He was standing on the leaf-strewn path which led up out of the valley to Bourne and the world beyond. He could not see his crystal ball—but perhaps it was somewhere there in the dead leaves, at the threshold of the secret country. Or perhaps the river boy had kept it, as

Nathaniel had wished him to. He looked back once more at the Pole Star. Then, comforted by its friendly shining, he set out. It was time to be gone; for tomorrow he had a new journey before him.